Charles Willeby

Frederic François Chopin

Charles Willeby

Frederic François Chopin

ISBN/EAN: 9783742891471

Manufactured in Europe, USA, Canada, Australia, Japa

Cover: Foto ©Raphael Reischuk / pixelio.de

Manufactured and distributed by brebook publishing software
(www.brebook.com)

Charles Willeby

Frederic François Chopin

PREFACE

So much has already been written concerning Frederic Chopin and his work, that it would at first sight seem unnecessary to add further to the list. Nevertheless, it is only quite recently that the truth concerning many points in his career has come to light. Moreover, a great part of the Chopin literature is so highly coloured and overdrawn, and contains so little that is reliable as to render it practically worthless. Therefore I have endeavoured to put forward a true, concise, and unexaggerated account of the composer's life, and to point out some of the most characteristic features of his work. To assist me towards the accomplishment of the first of these endeavours, I have had the valuable assistance of, amongst others, Professor Niecks's excellent and comprehensive *Life of Chopin,* which is the most recent and exhaustive of the works on this musician. Further, my information has been derived from newspapers, magazines, foreign biographies, and from correspondence with a few of those who had the good fortune to make the master's acquaintance either abroad, or during the short time he spent in this country. The line of action which I have adopted with regard to the analysis of the works is neither wholly technical nor wholly emotional. Whatever the matter under discussion best admitted of, and whatever seemed to me most necessary, I have endeavoured to supply. In conclusion, while expressing my obligations to the authors and publishers of those works (a list of which is appended) to which I have referred, I may state that I have used almost exclusively Messrs. Breitkopf & Härtel's edition of Chopin's complete works, except in such cases as where it has been necessary to compare the various texts.

CHARLES WILLEBY.

LONDON, 14*th February* 1892.

LIST OF WORKS CONSULTED

Frederic Chopin as a Man and Musician. By FREDERICK NIECKS. (London: Novello, Ewer & Co.)

Chopin, and other Musical Essays. By HENRY T. FINCK. (London: T. Fisher Unwin.)

Frederic Chopin. By FRANZ LISZT, translated by M. W. COOK. (London: W. Reeves.)

Life and Letters of Frederic Chopin. By MORITZ KARASOWSKI, translated from the German by EMILY HILL. (London: W. Reeves.)

The Works of Frederic Chopin, and their Proper Interpretation. By JEAN KLECZYNSKI, translated by A. WHITTINGHAM. (London: W. Reeves.)

Musical Studies. By FRANCIS HUEFFER. (Edinburgh: A. & C. Black.)

George Sand. By BERTHA THOMAS. (London: W. H. Allen & Co.)

Letters from Majorca. By CHARLES W. WOOD, F.R.G.S. (London: Bentley & Son.)

Frederic Chopin. By JOSEPH BENNETT. (Novello, Ewer & Co.)

Histoire de ma Vie and *Correspondance.* GEORGE SAND. (Paris: Calmann Lévy.)

Frédéric Chopin. Sa vie et ses œuvres. Par Mme. A. AUDLEY. (Paris: E. Plon et Cie.)

Les trois Romans de Frédéric Chopin. Par le Comte WODZINSKI. (Paris: Calmann Lévy.)

F. Chopin, Essai de Critique Musicale. Par H. BARBEDETTE. (Paris: Heugel et Cie.)

Les Musiciens Polonais. Par ALBERT SOWINSKI. (Paris: Le Clere, 1857.)

CONTENTS

CHAPTER I

CHAPTER XI

CHAPTER XII

CHAPTER XIII

CHAPTER XIV

CONCLUSION

FREDERIC FRANÇOIS CHOPIN

CHAPTER I

IT is the rule rather than the exception that the
nationality of a distinguished artist has a marked
bearing upon his art; but in no instance has this
rule been more forcibly exemplified than in that of
the subject of this biography. And seeing that this
is so, it will not be out of place, if, before proceeding to deal with the life of Frederic Chopin, we
endeavour to give the reader some slight idea of the
people from whom he sprung. As this digression
must of necessity be brief, we shall confine ourselves
the more particularly to that nation which seems
to have excited the most noticeable, if not the
greatest, influence upon his work,—for Frederic
Chopin had within him two distinct nationalities:
those of Poland and of France. The name Chopin

is by no means an uncommon one in the latter country, nor—apart from the bearer of it with whom we are now concerned—can it be said to be undistinguished; for by the efforts of René Chopin the *littérateur*, and Charles Auguste Chopin the poet, it was made, if not famous, sufficiently prominent. The original title of the family from which Chopin came was, no doubt, Chopin d'Arnouville, for a member of that family it was, who, a sufferer by the revocation of the Edict of Nantes, fled to Poland. And although there is much of uncertainty in connection with this, as with other theories concerning Chopin's ancestry, we can, by accepting it as correct, satisfactorily account for that part of the inscription on his tombstone which states him to be the *fils d'un émigré français.*

Another version is that Nicholas, the father of Frederic Chopin, was the natural son of a Polish nobleman who had accompanied King Stanislas to Lorraine, and had there taken the name of Chopin. Which of these two stories is the correct one we cannot tell, for we have little to guide us to a decision between them, but such facts as are at our command seem to point to the acceptance of the first theory. At all events, it is with the Poles and Poland that we propose briefly to deal. It was in the fifteenth and sixteenth centuries, while under the kings of the Jagellon dynasty, that Poland had its most brilliant epoch. Under these sovereigns they wrested from the Russians the provinces of Red Russia, Little Russia, and White Russia; from the Germans those of West and East Prussia, Courland, and Livonia; the result being that following these conquests there existed in Polish realm three nationalities, about four-eighths of the whole population being Russians, while three-eighths were Poles, and the one-eighth were Germans. As a consequence of this we have at the same time some five different religious confessions in Poland. The Orthodox Greeks, the United Greeks (by which is meant Catholics who, while acknowledging the Pope, observed the Greek ritual), the Roman Catholics, the Protestants of the Lutheran and those of the reformed Confession. Of these, the Russian subjects belonged to the Greek Church, the Germans being Protestants. In dealing with these conditions the Jagellons were highly successful, but such was unfortunately not the case with their successors. The nobles gradually encroached until at last all efforts were powerless to restrain them. They entirely overpowered all other classes, yet were incapable of forming themselves into anything approaching a stable Government.

To them belonged all lands that were not appropriated by the Church or by the State. Each noble considered himself a sovereign prince, and even judged himself empowered not only to contract alliances with foreign Powers, but to receive subsidies from them.

The full meaning of such a state of things we only grasp when we find that the nobility at that time constituted a fourteenth part of the population! Nor can we be surprised that under the circumstances those Russian and German subjects who were subjugated by the country had little to induce them to amalgamate with their rulers. The end of the sixteenth century witnessed in Poland a serious outbreak of religious strife. The Jesuits, who had obtained a powerful influence in the country, desired that the whole power of the State should be placed under the Romish Church, and that war should be declared against heresy, both in Poland and out of it. As a result of this, the country was involved in a series of disastrous wars against Russia and Sweden. The power of Poland was now well on the decline, and the realm became thoroughly demoralised; the culmination being reached in 1772, when the treaty of the First Partition of Poland was signed. This was no long-prepared scheme; on the contrary, it was a sudden expedient to avert a great European war, and its result, as regards the territories taken from Poland, was beneficial, inasmuch as it afforded escape from a hopeless state of anarchy which could not have been but disastrous. The Poles themselves had utterly destroyed their own commonwealth a considerable time before the schemes of 1770-72 were thought of.

As to the character of the people of Poland, it has always been remarkable for its brilliant qualities, prominent among which are an impetuous bravery, restless ambition, and great national pride. Coupled with these they possess a passionate excitability and a great susceptibility of all intellectual pleasure, while they have always been noted for their polish and amiability in social intercourse. In the possession of most of these qualities they would seem to be at one with the French; indeed they have been called the French of the north. Yet notwithstanding the great similarity between the two nations, in the many respects we have noted, there is a difference between them which is quite as forcibly marked; for while the highest ideal of the Pole is one of personal freedom from any political restraint, two very characteristic points in the French nature are national unity and great military discipline.

Frederick II. does not spare the Poles, whom he describes as capable of anything for the sake of money, frivolous, lacking in judgment, and who, he says, are equally ready to join or abandon a party without any adequate reason. Exaggerated as these animadversions on the Polish character doubtless are, there is not lacking in them much that is true. Certain it is that we can find prominent instances without number of the first of the charges which he makes against them. We have already touched on the lack of material at hand to guide us to the truth concerning the ancestry of Chopin, and even the separating of the tares from the wheat, in that which we have, is a matter of no small difficulty. Therefore we do not propose to go into the matter here, but content ourselves with taking for our starting-point the birth of Chopin's father, Nicholas Chopin, which took place at Nancy, in Lorraine, on the 17th August 1770. Of his early youth little is known, but in his seventeenth year we find him putting into execution a desire which had gradually grown upon him to visit Poland. There are several reasons, either of which would satisfactorily account for this action on his part. The first is that if he were, as we have put forward, of Polish descent, he would only be carrying out, in this desire to visit his native land, a very marked characteristic of his countrymen. The second is, while more lengthy, none the less satisfactory. By the peace of Vienna in 1735 the Duchies of Lorraine and Bar passed into the possession of Stanislas Leszczynski, who had reigned as King of Poland from 1704-1709. He continued to reign over the above-named Duchies until his demise, which occurred in 1766. During the thirty years of his reign Stanislas had done much for his subjects, and the recollections of these good things did not die with him; on the contrary, they were still fresh in the minds of many Lorrainers when Nicholas Chopin saw the light. Nancy had consequently become a kind of half-way house to the many Polish travellers on their way to Paris; while the kindly remembrance of their late monarch engendered a desire on the part of many of those Poles, resident in the Duchies, to visit their native land. Thus it may have been that Nicholas came to Warsaw.

But another and perhaps more sordid reason seems to us to have put at all events the much desired visit into actual accomplishment. A friend of Nicholas Chopin had left Lorraine some time previously with the object of establishing in Warsaw a tobacco manufactory, in order that he might profit by the rapidly increasing habit of snuff-taking. His venture turning out highly successful, he remembered his friend Nicholas, and offered him the charge of the book-keeping in his business. This offer, as was to be expected, Nicholas eagerly accepted, and as a result we find him in Warsaw in 1787.

At the time of his arrival the Poles were anxiously

awaiting the assembly of the Diet which was to take place in the following year for the purpose of preventing the excessive use of the *liberum veto.* Nicholas Chopin threw himself heart and soul into the affairs of the country, which for the next twenty years were hopelessly complicated. During this time Poland suffered much at the hand of both Prussia and Russia, especially the latter. Under Kósciuszko the people fought valiantly for their outraged country, but the powers against them were too strong, and the struggle was horribly ended by the siege and fall of Praga (a suburb of Warsaw) and the massacre which followed it.

After the third partition in 1795, Poland as a country disappeared. All this had naturally an effect the reverse of beneficial to trade, and among the sufferers in this respect was the friend of Nicholas, who was obliged to close his tobacco manufactory. This occurred shortly before the disastrous finale of which we have just spoken, that is in 1794, when the injured people were preparing for their gallant struggle, and were rallying their forces under the generalship of Kósciuszko. Nicholas Chopin being thrown out of his employment, joined the National Guard, in which he soon attained the rank of captain, and was present at the siege of Praga. At the end of the war he deliberated as to whether he should return to France or remain in Poland. The problem was solved for him, for he fell ill and was unable to move.

When he recovered he endeavoured to procure pupils, a thorough knowledge of the French language being the only available stock-in-trade he possessed. This proved of value to him, although not exactly in the way he had looked for. The Staroscina [1] Laszynska (whom Karasowski says he had met previously at Nancy) now offered him the post of tutor to her family, which consisted of two girls and two boys. In this position he remained for some time, only leaving it to undertake a similar one in the household of the Countess Skarbek. This lady lived at Zelazowa-Wola, a village situated near the gates of Warsaw. Without being wealthy she was possessed of considerable means, and maintained a fairly large establishment. Nicholas Chopin's duty would seem to

---

[1] A Staroscina is the wife of a Starosta—*i.e.* a nobleman upon whom a castle and domains have been conferred by the crown.

have been particularly light, for instead of four pupils he had but one, the Countess's son Frederick; while his relations with his employer and her family were, and always continued to be, most cordial. At all events he found sufficient time to fall in love, the object of his affections being a young *protégée* of the Count's, by name Justina Krzyzanowska. This lady, who came of a noble but correspondingly poor family, he ultimately married in the spring of the year 1806. By her he had four children, one son and three daughters. The first child, Louisa, was born in April 1807. She turned her thoughts in the direction of literature, contributing to several periodicals, and also writing several books alone, and later in collaboration with her sister Isabella. She married Professor Jedrzejcaricz, and died in 1855. The second daughter, Isabella, married Anton Barcinski, an inspector of schools, who only died as recently as 1881. Thus in 1808 we find Nicholas Chopin with two daughters, and a consequent desire to obtain possession of an independent income.

As a teacher he was certainly justified in considering himself successful, and Count Skarbek, in his

Memoirs, has spoken of his son's tutor in the highest terms. That he did not do so without good reason is apparent from the fact that young Frederick Skarbek proved a brilliant pupil, distinguishing himself in poetry and science, and ultimately becoming a Professor in the University of Warsaw.

As a man, Nicholas Chopin was blessed with one of the most precious of Nature's gifts—sound common-sense. A charitable man, as well as a man of culture, he made many influential friends in the world of literature and art. For his wife, the very high estimation in which she was held, and the love and affection which was given her by her children, speaks much. She has been described as 'particularly tender-hearted and rich in all true womanly virtues,' and was, as Chopin calls her in his letters, 'the best of mothers.' They were a family united as one. Their life was simple and intellectual, their interests bound up in one another, and, although poor, they never lacked the necessaries of life, nor felt in any way the privations of poverty. Such, then, was the family into which our Frederick had the good fortune to be born.

The birth of the son who was to make the name of Chopin famous, took place in their little house at Zelazowa-Wola on 1st March 1809. But here they were not to remain for long, for in the following year the good opinion of Nicholas Chopin, held by Count Skarbek, was endorsed by the Directors of the Warsaw Lyceum, who gave practical expression to it by appointing him Professor of the French language at that newly-founded institution. This necessitated a removal into Warsaw. The immediate benefit of his appointment was not great to the Professor, for it entailed the additional expenses of a town life; but in the year following, the offer of a similar position in the School of Artillery and Engineering considerably facilitated matters.

The little Frederic duly received the name of Frederic François, after the son of Count Skarbek, who stood as his godfather. We are told that he very soon showed a great susceptibility to musical sounds, although hardly in the direction which we should have expected, for he howled lustily whenever he heard them. But as this seems not uncommon amongst babies as a class, it is hardly worth any serious consideration. At all events he soon dismissed any impression which he may have caused, that music was in any way distasteful to him, for he took to the pianoforte (to use a vulgar phrase) as a duck does to water. His parents being, as we have seen, blessed with intellect and sound common-sense, did not attempt to dissuade him from it, but placed him, young as he was, for instruction, in the art, under one of the best of its masters. To them, for this action we cannot be sufficiently thankful, for although the result would probably have been much the same had they waited a year or two, we cannot over-estimate the great value of musical guidance to one so young, for on the early musical food of the musician much depends.

The master chosen for the boy in pianoforte playing was Adalbert Zywny, a Bohemian, who had settled in Warsaw and established a good practice as a teacher, and whatever he may have been as a performer on his own instrument, in this capacity he was without a rival in the Polish capital. Chopin's opinion of him was always of the highest, and there is no doubt that he was more suitable as a teacher than would

have been one who might, perhaps, have possessed
higher capabilities as a pianist. For he instructed
and thoroughly grounded his young pupil in the
rudiments of his art, which in itself did much to
establish a sure and sound basis. As a proof of his
progress young Frederic at nine years of age showed
signs of becoming what Mr. Joseph Bennett, in his
short biography of him, calls 'that usually objection-
able thing, an "infant phenomenon."' A Polish lady
who heard him play at a soirée when not nine years
of age spoke of him as 'a child who, in the opinion
of connoisseurs of the art promised to replace Mozart.'
During his ninth year he was invited to assist at a
concert which had been got up by several influential
personages for the benefit of the poor. With the
concurrence of his master Frederic accepted the
invitation and played a pianoforte concerto, the
composition of Adalbert Gyrowetz,[1] a famous composer at the time. Karasowski's relation of this is
worthy of note :—'A few hours before the performance

---

[1] Adalbert Gyrowetz was a Bohemian. He was born at Budweis
in 1763,—was a conspicuous figure in London in 1789, and was the
composer of some thirty operas and a quantity of chamber music.
He died in Vienna in 1850.

Fritzchen, as he was called at home, was placed on a chair to be suitably dressed for his first appearance before a large assembly. The child was delighted with his jacket, and especially with the handsome collar. After the concert, his mother, who had not been present, asked, as she embraced him, " What did the public like best?" He naïvely answered, " Oh, mamma, everybody looked only at my collar." '

After the complete and emphatic success of his *début*, the little Frederic became the adored of the aristocracy of Warsaw, visiting frequently such houses as those of the Princes Czartoryski, Lubecki, Radziwill and others. Not content with his pianoforte studies, Chopin early essayed musical composition. These youthful efforts generally took the form of dances such as waltzes, mazurkas, and polonaises. When ten years of age he dedicated a march which he had composed to the Grand Duke Constantine, who had it scored for, and played by, one of the military bands. His father now very wisely determined that his son should receive instruction in the grammar of his art, simultaneously with his pianoforte instruction. Alas! how rarely such a course is adopted even to-day; and we venture to say in passing, that if the adoption of it were more general amongst our young amateurs, the frequent aspersions now cast upon our national musical reputation would decrease very materially both in number and severity.

Here it was again necessary to obtain an efficient master, and fortune so far aided circumspection on the part of Nicholas Chopin as to bring him in contact with a master in every way worthy of directing the genius which already showed itself in the youthful musician. As Joseph Elsner was a conspicuous figure, not only by virtue of his position as Chopin's only master in harmony and counterpoint, but on his own account, we can, without apology, turn our attention briefly upon him. Elsner, we are told, while the son of a cabinetmaker, was intended for the medical profession, and with that object was sent to school at Breslau, and later for the completion of his studies to the University at Vienna. A native of Silesia, his father was resident at Grodgrau. In this city the lad had received much encouragement from his friends to cultivate his voice, and consequently, upon arriving in Breslau, he joined one of the best church choirs there. His love of music gradually obtaining a stronger hold of him, he quite abandoned his intention of becoming a doctor. He became in turn conductor of the theatres of Lemberg and Warsaw. As a composer he was highly productive, as will be seen when we state that he composed as many as twenty-two operas in the space of twenty years, and, moreover, we have good reason to believe that his work was little less conspicuous from a qualitative than from a quantitative point of view. In Warsaw he was highly valued and much liked, and his influence on the cultivation of his art in his country was by no means small; indeed, he has been, perhaps, not unfitly named the 'ancestor of modern Polish music.' Among his most successful works we may name his *Echo Variations for the Orchestra*, and his Oratorio, *The Passion of the Saviour*. Besides these, he wrote many symphonies and a quantity of chamber music. One of his greatest ambitions was reached when, in 1825, he was appointed to the Directorship of the Warsaw Conservatoire of Music. Also prominent amongst his pupils must be named a famous Polish musician — Charles Kurpinski. In short,

Joseph Elsner was a thoroughly capable musician, who, if only a man of talent, was perhaps for that very reason exactly what was needed for the careful guidance of a young genius. But to return to our subject. We must not omit to chronicle a very marked expression of recognition of young Chopin's unusual capabilities, made by the celebrated vocalist Madame Catalani, upon whom the young artist had evidently made a great impression. It took the very handsome form of a gold watch, on which was inscribed, ' Donné par Madame Catalani à Frederic Chopin, âgé de dix ans.'

Some five years after the birth of Frederic, a third daughter was born to Nicholas Chopin and his wife. This daughter, Emilia, who unfortunately died at the early age of fourteen, gave promise of very great things in the province of literature, and besides being exceptionally gifted, she is described as having had a highly attractive personality and great ambition. It certainly says much for her that she was, in the short time allotted to her, sufficiently clever and industrious to have translated many of the works of the German author, Salzmann.

Moreover, her poetical efforts augured well for her future, and there can be no doubt that, had she lived, she would have occupied no unworthy place in the world of literature.

We have now some idea of the career before our young artist, and of the conditions under which it began; and having thus followed him to the end of the first decade of his life, we shall in the next chapter touch upon some of the characteristics which were prominent features of his personality.

CHAPTER II

As we stated in the prefatory note to this work
much has been written concerning Chopin which is
not only misleading but absolutely incorrect. Much,
also, has been written that is rhapsodical and exaggerated, and, as a natural result thereof, we find that
there exists in the minds of many a total misappre-
hension of the physical aspect and character of Chopin
both in his boyhood and during his manhood. In his
youth he has been described to us as 'a little creature
who suffered much yet ever tried to smile,' and
'whose friends were so glad that he did not become
moody or morose, that they were satisfied to cherish
his good qualities, believing that he opened his heart
to them without reserve and gave to them all his
secret thoughts'; this, says, Karasowski, is Liszt's description of the boy. But here the Polish biographer
has not adhered to the facts of the case, as this picture

of Chopin was taken by Liszt from George Sand's description of Prince Karol[1] in her novel *Lucrezia Floriani*. We agree that Liszt was no biographer. Moreover, even if he had possessed the necessary qualities for writing an uncoloured account of Chopin's life, the fact remains that he did not make the composer's acquaintance until comparatively late in his life. Moreover, we know that much of the information provided by Liszt was supplied him by the Pole, Albert Grzymala, who did not meet Chopin until the latter came to Paris to live. Therefore Liszt's book is, at all events as regards the early part of the composer's career, comparatively useless to us. George Sand— even if we take it for granted that Prince Karol is an intended portrayal of Chopin—cannot be taken to task for in ever so slight a degree diverging from facts, for we have always to remember the wide gulf which separates fact from fiction, at all events in this respect. Nor is Karasowski, in his anxiety to depict Chopin as robust, justified in quoting this utterance of the novelist as coming originally from Liszt. Chopin was, in his youth, undoubtedly delicate, but he was

---

[1] Supposed to be Chopin.

healthy and bright, although in no way 'vigorous.' This was only natural, as we can understand when we know that his sister Amelia and his father were both the victims of pulmonary disease. But, on the other hand, Karasowski is quite right in asserting that he was far from being the sickly, sentimental child which he has been stated to have been. His pleasures were intellectual rather than physical, and, being delicate, he was wise in taking great care of his health, especially when the disease to which he was predisposed is one which misses no opportunity to seize its unhappy victim. His parents, knowing this, were doubly careful with him, and doubtless did err (if it can be said under the circumstances to be erring) on the side of 'coddling' him; but, nevertheless, it had this good result: that up to the time of his manhood Chopin was only once ill.

Up to the age of fifteen he was taught at home in company with his father's pupils, and made such good progress that, when he entered the Warsaw Lyceum, he was able to take a high place in the school. Here, again, Liszt goes astray, for he states confidently that Frederic's education was due to the kindness and intelligent protection of Prince Anton Radziwill. Even had this statement not received a flat denial by Chopin's relatives, it would surely seem highly improbable to any one acquainted with Nicholas Chopin's position as a professor in Warsaw, especially when there is no mention of anything of the kind in any of his letters.

At school Frederic was a prime favourite, and was always in the midst of any fun or mischief which was going on, while at home, although his energies were directed in a more desirable direction, they were none the less marked. His talent for mimicry was always extraordinary, and has been commented upon not only by George Sand and Liszt, but by Balzac. On the birthdays of their parents the Chopin family devoted themselves to giving amateur theatrical performances, and in these Frederic was invariably the prime mover, and on one occasion he not only acted in, but wrote in collaboration with his sister, a one-act comedy in verse, entitled *The Mistake*. He would seem to have exhibited a natural aptitude for the stage; indeed, one Polish actor who frequently assisted the young amateur on these occasions went so far as to say that Chopin was born to be a great actor.

Amongst the visitors and friends of Nicholas Chopin at this time must be mentioned Dr. Samuel Linde, the rector of the Lyceum, and a distinguished philologist, Casimir Brodzinski a famous Polish poet and *littérateur*, with marked tendencies towards the romantic in art; his former pupil, Count Frederic Skarbek, now a University professor, and many others, all men of learning, if not of note. Thus it will be seen that the home influence of our young artist was highly refining, and amidst such surrounding his naturally artistic tendencies greatly developed, and at the Lyceum he made rapid progress. His holidays were mostly spent in the country, and generally at the village of Szafarnia, which belonged to the Dziewanowski family, with whom he formed a firm friendship.

Karasowski relates how, while spending one of his holidays at this place, Chopin conceived the idea of 'bringing out a small manuscript newspaper,' which he entitled the *Szafarnia Courier* after the pattern of the *Warsaw Courier*, to take the place of his ordinary home-letters. In this he would write all that was happening in the neighbourhood, and frequently inserted an account of his artistic doings after the following manner :—'On July 15th M. Pichon [a name he assumed] appeared at the musical assembly at Szafarnia, at which were present several persons, big, and little : he played Kalkbrenner's Concerto, but this did not produce such a *furore*, especially among the youthful hearers, as did the song which he rendered.' The same biographer also puts it forward as specially illustrative of a custom prevailing in Warsaw, that this miniature journal of Chopin's had to be examined by the Government censor, whose duty it was to write across every number ' lawful for transmission.' When we are told that at the time this office was held by Mlle. Louise Dziewanowski we can readily understand that in Chopin's case this ' red-tapeism ' was in no way irksome either to the lady or to him.

Another anecdote of the boy at this time, and one which sufficiently illustrates the spirit of mischief within him, has been told. At the neighbouring village of Obcrów were a number of Jews, whom young Frederic frequently used to delight with his playing. One of them, a M. Romecki, had sold a quantity of grain to a dealer. Frederic, having heard of this, sent the former gentleman a letter purporting to come from the grain-dealer, to the effect that, after having duly considered the matter, he had decided not to complete the purchase. His imitation of the language in use amongst these Polish Jews was so good that the unfortunate Romecki was completely taken in. His rage can easier be imagined than described, and the catastrophe which would inevitably have occurred was only prevented by the timely confession of the young miscreant. But it is only fair to our young artist to follow this anecdote with one which can in no way be prejudicial to him. The story is told by Casimir Wodzynski, and is harmless enough, still it serves to show at what an early age the young musician indulged in improvisation.

I will quote from Karasowski:—'If his father's pupils made too great a noise in the house Frederic had but to seat himself at the piano to obtain perfect quiet. One day, during the professor's absence, there was an uproarious scene, and Barcinski, the assistant master, was at his wits' end as to what to do, when Frederic fortunately entered the room. Without delay he requested the offenders to sit down, and calling in those who were making a noise outside, he promised to improvise a story on the piano if they would be quiet. This at once had the desired effect, and having extinguished the lights he began. He described how robbers set out to plunder a house, and arrived, then proceeded to enter by means of ladders to the windows. Suddenly startled by a noise from within they fled into the woods, where they are supposed to have fallen asleep. To illustrate this he played more and more softly a slow, rocking movement, until (we are told) his hearers had actually themselves fallen asleep. Seeing this, Frederic noiselessly crept out of the room to his parents and sisters, whom he requested to follow him with a light. When the astonished family had duly comprehended the state of affairs, he, with a crashing chord, awoke the sleepers, who naturally were considerably startled, and we trust somewhat repentant.' Touching upon his marvellous powers of improvisation, Karasowski speaks of Chopin's 'profound knowledge of counterpoint, but we doubt whether this is the correct expression for his aptitude in that branch of the art. Such counterpoint as is illustrated in his work either early or late does not impress us as being the result of profound knowledge.' It is more the counterpoint of the genius than of the student. Certain it is that he frequently transgresses many of its primary laws, but even if he did this to suit his artistic purpose (as no doubt in many instances he did), we must take into consideration the fact that counterpoint was by no means fluent even in the work of Elsner; on the contrary, his master was frequently taken to task by critics and musicians for his laxity in this direction. Chopin, in his youth, would seem to have in some degree exhibited that waywardness and irregularity which is duly expected from 'genius.' He had a small piano in his bedroom, and would frequently wake in the middle of the night with some phrase in his head, which he would straightway proceed to play on the instrument, or some discord which, to enable him the more clearly to understand it, he would resolve. Karasowski follows this statement with another, to the effect that he was much loved by the servants in the house, which, we think, would have come better before it than after. They, he says, shook their heads saying, 'The poor young gentleman's mind is affected.'

On May 27th and June 10th in the year 1825, Chopin played at two concerts given in the large hall of the Conservatoire in Warsaw. On these occasions he gave Moscheles' Concerto in G minor, and also some improvisations. The only critique of the concerts which was written spoke of him as having a wealth of musical ideas and being a master of his instrument, which is indeed high praise for one so young.

In this same year he published his Opus 1; this was a Rondo in C minor. But on reference to the posthumous publications contained in our catalogue, it will be seen that there is a polonaise in G sharp minor, bearing the date of composition 1822. This is the date given in Messrs. Breitkopf's edition, and, moreover, on the Warsaw edition is the following note :—'So far as one can judge from the manuscript and its dedication, this composition was written by Frederic Chopin at the age of fourteen, and never published until now.' But this is by no means convincing, and a careful examination of the work itself certainly inclines us to believe that it must have been composed considerably later.

Chopin had now discontinued his pianoforte study under Zwyny, and devoted his time mainly to composition. Nevertheless, his playing made rapid strides. The 'school' of that time was quite insufficient for his requirements, and necessity, being the mother of invention, caused him gradually to create those innovations in pianoforte technique which were even later looked upon as heretical. He was, as can be imagined, a great favourite in all the 'salons' of Warsaw, and this fact again Liszt seizes upon with avidity as forming an admirable opportunity for that 'gush' to which he was so addicted. 'Chopin,' he says, 'could easily read the hearts which were attracted to him by friendship and the grace of his youth, and thus was enabled early to learn of what a strange mixture of leaven and cream of roses, of gunpowder and tears of angels, the poetic ideal of his nation is formed. When his wandering fingers ran over the keys, suddenly touching some moving chords, he could see how the furtive tears coursed down the cheeks of the loving girl, or the young neglected wife; how they moistened the eyes of the young men, enamoured of and eager for glory. Can we not fancy some young beauty asking him to play a simple prelude, then, softened by the tones, leaning her rounded arms upon the instrument, to support her dreaming head, while she suffered the young artist to divine in the dewy glitter of her lustrous eyes the song sung by her youthful heart?' This speaks for itself, and is only one of many similar passages to be found in the great pianist's 'rhapsody.'

Frederic now worked very hard, and when in 1826 his sister Emilia was ordered by the doctors to Reinerz, a watering-place in Silesia, it was decided that he should accompany her, and endeavour to regain his health, which was rapidly becoming affected by his constant application to study. His stay at this watering-place, although a short one, had in a great measure the desired effect, and his letters to his friend William Kolberg are particularly bright.

He benefited the more from his entire cessation of all mental work, and his only musical activity took the benevolent direction of giving two concerts in aid of two orphans, who having, like himself, come to the town to benefit their health, had, by the death of their mother, no means of support, and not even sufficient money to defray the funeral expenses. The remainder of his holidays Frederic passed chiefly at Strzyzewo, the property of his godmother, Madame Wiesiolawska. While there he took advantage of the close proximity of Prince Anton Radziwill's country seat to accept an invitation extended to him by that nobleman, to visit him. Prince Radziwill, although related to the Prussian royal family, had property and numerous friends in Poland, and spent no small part of his time in the country. A musician himself, he had felt a special interest in the young prodigy of whom everyone was talking. That he was in no way disappointed in the expectation he had formed of Frederic we may conclude by his actions later, for when, some three years afterwards, he represented Prussia at the coronation of the Polish king, Nicholas I., he visited Chopin, and invited him to Posen, of which duchy he was the governor. The prince was no mere *dilettante*, as is proved by the serious work to which he applied himself; he was not only a good singer and 'cellist, but his compositions were noted for their refinement and thorough musicianship; while as regards the height of his ambitions, we have only to mention the fact that he chose the first portion of Goethe's *Faust* as a subject for musical setting.[1] We have already dealt with the statement regarding the prince's contribution towards the education of the young artist as improbable, but nevertheless when we see and take into consideration his high position, and his love for, and thorough knowledge of, the art of music, we can readily understand that he was in many ways—although probably indirectly—of great assistance to Chopin. Later on we shall have occasion to refer to the happy intervention of the prince at a juncture when, without it, the career of the young musician would seem likely to have been cut short.

It must not be forgotten that, up to this time, there was no definite intention on the part of Chopin's parents that their son should take up music

---

[1] Prince Radziwill's *Faust* was privately performed in London in 1880.

as a profession. They had, although expressing no wish that he should not do so, remained entirely passive in the matter. But the young musician's success both in pianoforte playing and composition was so great, that when the persuasions of his master were brought to bear upon the matter, little objection was raised by them.

He had now left the Lyceum, and, as a result of his greater application to music, did not come through the ordeal of his final examination so successfully as might have been expected from his previous performances. Henceforth, then, Chopin was at liberty to devote himself entirely to his art; and as we are now about to enter upon that period of his life which was devoted to artistic and professional travels, we shall close this chapter with a glance at his compositions up to this time. The Rondo Op. 1 is dedicated to Madame Linde, wife of the rector, Dr. Linde, whom we mentioned as the friend of Nicholas Chopin. It is a highly creditable composition when we consider the boy's age, and it could not reasonably be expected to show any emphatic signs of originality. Nevertheless, there is no small amount of inventive power demonstrated, and it is a work to which the composer could look back in after years without any sense of shame as his Op. 1. The following Op. 2, however, shows a very great advance upon it, and evinces distinct signs of originality, although they are more in the 'design' of the pianoforte figures than in musical thought. The variations of Mozart's captivating melody are inventive, and, above all, Chopin clearly demonstrates his knowledge of the resources of his instrument. Robert Schumann's criticism of this Op. 2 may be summed up by quoting the exclamation to which he gave vent on reading the work :—'Hats off, gentlemen: a genius!' Through all the 'virtuosity' in this composition, Schumann recognised those dormant qualities which afterwards awoke to such good purpose.

The Op. 3., Introduction and Polonaise for pianoforte and violoncello, was written while staying at the house of Prince Radziwill, who was, as we know, a performer upon the 'cello. In a letter written about October 1829, Chopin speaks of it as an *Alla Polacca*, at the same time stating that it was intended for nothing more than a showy 'salon piece, such as will please ladies.' This, of course, disarms all serious criticism, and we shall content ourselves with noting a few of the most prominent features of this somewhat commonplace effort. The Introduction opens with a short prelude for the pianoforte. This is followed by the initial theme for the violoncello, which forms the movement of the Introduction. At the end of the movement the composer does not come to a close on the tonic, but branches off on the dominant through a brilliant cadenza to the Polacca theme, this commonplace melody being given to the 'cello. The only portion of the work which seems to us to be in any degree worthy of its composer is the counter theme for the violoncello in the key of F major. This, with its brilliant pianoforte accompaniment, is the only redeeming feature of the piece.

We may now fitly close with the three Polonaises written in this early period, and published posthumously by Julius Fontana. The first in D minor, written in 1827, is the most spontaneous of all the early compositions. Here we find, in embryo, many of those Chopinesque turns by which we afterwards learn to know the master. The accompanying two, in B flat major and F minor respectively, while exhibiting no less emotional power, do not strike us as so spontaneous as that in D minor, which is a truly wonderful performance, when we consider the composer's short experience. From this time forward his work will be seen to gain more repose, and that sense of superfluity which so characterises these early efforts is gradually thrown off. Moreover, as we proceed, the poetic and emotional elements take entire precedence over that of virtuosity (except, perhaps, in the case of one or two of the large works for piano and orchestra), and all that we term Chopinesque is gradually unfolded to us, while with it is no less distinctly revealed the personality of the man. Having thus briefly glanced at the efforts of what we might almost term his childhood, let us now take up the thread of our narrative, and prepare to follow our young artist on his travels.

CHAPTER III

THE first journey of our young artist was an important break in the uneventful quietude of his former life. He was, however, fortunate in having the companionship of a cultured man and friend of his father in Dr. Jarocki. The professor was visiting Berlin at the invitation of the Berlin University, Frederick William III. of Prussia having desired that a Congress should be held, and all the most eminent philosophers invited to attend. At the proposal that his young friend should accompany him, the professor expressed himself delighted, and on the 9th September 1828 they left Warsaw. After five days' posting they arrived at their destination, and took up their quarters at the hotel 'Kronprinz.' And now I shall let our young friend speak for himself :—

'MY DEARLY BELOVED PARENTS AND SISTERS,—We arrived safely in this great city about three o'clock on Sunday afternoon, and went direct from the port to the hotel 'Kronprinz,' where we are still. It is a good and comfortable house. The day of our arrival Professor Jarocki took me to Herr Lichtenstein's, where I met Alex. von Humboldt. He is not above the middle height, and his features cannot be called handsome; but the prominent brow, and the deep, penetrating glance reveal the searching intellect of the scholar, who is as great a philanthropist as he is a traveller. He speaks French like his mother tongue; even you would say so, dear father . . . . There is a rumour that the great Paganini is coming here. I only hope it is true. Prince Radziwill is expected on the 20th of this month. It will be a great pleasure to me if he comes. I have as yet seen nothing but the Zoological Cabinet, but I know the city pretty well, for I wandered among the beautiful streets and bridges for two whole days. . . . The chief impression Berlin makes upon me is that of a straggling city, which could, I think, contain double its present large population. To-day will be my first experience of the music of Berlin. Do not think me one-sided, dearest father, if I say that I would much rather have spent the morning at Schlesinger's than in labouring through the thirteen rooms of the Zoological Museum; but I came here for the sake of my musical education, and Schlesinger's library, containing, as it does, the most important musical works of every age and country, is, of course, of more interest to me than any other collection. I console myself with the thought that I shall not miss Schlesinger's, and that a young man ought to see all he can, as there is something to be learnt everywhere.

'. . . The Prussian diligences are most uncomfortable, so

the journey was less agreeable than I had looked for; however, I reached the capital of the Hohenzollerns in good health and spirits. Our travelling companions were a German lawyer living at Posen, who tried to distinguish himself by making coarse jokes; and a very fat farmer with a smattering of politeness acquired by travelling. At the last stage before Frankfort-on-the-Oder, a German Sappho entered the diligence and poured forth a torrent of ridiculous egotistical complaints. Quite unwittingly the good lady amused me immensely, for it was as good as a comedy when she began to argue with the lawyer, who, instead of laughing at her, seriously controverted everything she said . . . Marylski cannot have an atom of taste if he thinks the Berlin ladies dress well; their clothes are handsome, no doubt, but, alas! for the beautiful stuffs cut up for such puppets!—Your ever fondly loving

'FREDERIC.'

There is, we think, in this letter not only a considerable fund of humour, but an observation of men and things remarkable in a young man of his age. Here it is, perhaps, that there is a slight similarity between Chopin and Mendelssohn, for although the letters of the latter are much more direct and decided, especially when speaking of music, there is to be found in them the same keen observance of the manners of men. In another letter, written shortly after the above, Chopin relates that he heard at the opera *Il Matrimonio Segreto* and Onslow's *Der Hausirer*. These performances, he says, he greatly enjoyed, but he appears to have been quite carried away by a performance of Handel's *Ode to St. Cecilia's Day*, which he describes as his 'ideal of sublime music.' In the same letter he says, speaking of the Congress:—'Spontini, Zelter, and Felix Mendelssohn Bartholdy were also there; but I did not speak to any of them, as I did not think it proper to introduce myself. It is said that Prince Radziwill will come to-day; I shall find out after breakfast if this is really true.' Unfortunately for Chopin, Prince Radziwill did not arrive that day, nor, so far as we can ascertain, did he arrive at all. Had he done so, many things might have been greatly facilitated for Chopin, for the prince was acquainted, and in some cases very intimate, with the shining lights in the musical world of Berlin; prominent amongst whom were Spontini and Ludwig Berger, the teacher of Mendelssohn.

It is strange how little touching on his art is to be found in Chopin's letters; moreover, in them we look in vain for those qualities portrayed in his music, and it is no exaggeration to say that we get a much truer picture of the man from his compositions than from any of his correspondence. This strikes us as the more extraordinary when we consider that Chopin was a contemporary of those musicians who were equally at their ease either with the pen of the author or the composer. For example, we have only to name Schumann and Wagner; and even Mendelssohn's letters are very much more reflective of their author than those of Chopin. Again, they are not what we should have expected from one who had received the careful and thorough literary training, not to speak of that higher education which is to be got from mixing with the cultured and intelligent people whom we know Frederic did mix with in the Polish capital. Of course, the fact must not be lost sight of that these letters are only written in a confidential vein to his parents and intimate friends, nor should we forget that they were written while he was still very young. But we doubt very much, had his Parisian correspondence not been destroyed, whether we should have found it to contain any of those qualities which would make it valuable apart from bearing his signature, save that one or two points about which we are now in the dark would perhaps have been satisfactorily disposed of. He undoubtedly found in his music a full and adequate means for the expression of all that he felt. In a word, his correspondence has but small claim to be called literary. What power of observation he possessed was, as we have seen, in the direction of dress and manners, or any special eccentricity. And he was not without a very strong vein of satire. Both of these qualities he frequently exerted in a very marked degree, and with age his satirical propensities increased.

A characteristic, perhaps it might even be called a peculiarity, upon which we have not touched, was his love of caricature. For the exercise of this gift his attendance at the Congress afforded him ample opportunity, which he in no way failed to take advantage of, for, as he said, he found so many unique specimens that he was obliged not only to sketch them but to classify them.

After a stay of some fourteen days in Berlin,

Chopin and the professor turned their steps homewards on 28th September 1828, breaking their journey at Posen, by the invitation of the Archbishop Wolicki. And here we have an anecdote to relate. Arrived at a small village named Züllichau, midway between Frankfort-on-Oder and Posen, they found they would have an hour to wait for horses, and in order the quicker to while away the time, the professor proposed a walk through the village. On this proposal they acted, but on their return they found no further signs of activity than when they had left. The professor, being also a philosopher, bethought himself of his inner man, and having ordered something in the way of refreshment proceeded to enjoy it. Not so Chopin. At all events his refreshment took an entirely different form, for in an adjoining room he had found a piano. The reader, knowing this, will hardly need to be told that, no sooner did he see it, than he sat down and commenced to play. He had now reason to be considerably more astonished than he had been on discovering its presence, for, *mirabile dictu*, it was in tune. Gradually attracted by the music, the postmaster, his buxom wife, and all the passengers dropped in. But Frederic was by this time quite unmindful of all that was taking place around him, and was deep in his improvisation. Everyone was likewise absorbed, and listening in rapt attention to wonderful tones produced by the young pianist, when suddenly a stentorian voice gave forth, 'The horses are ready, gentlemen.' So enraged was the postmaster at this untimely interruption, that he indulged in an epithet which, in his own language, appears to be so strong that we refrain from attempting its translation. Chopin had now got up from the piano, and was being pressed on all sides to continue his playing, the postmaster going so far as to offer extra horses to make up for the time they might lose by the delay. At length, overcome by their entreaties, he sat down and resumed his fantasia. When he had finished, the host sent in wines, and his daughters, we are told, served Chopin first. The host having proposed the toast of 'the favourite of Polyhymnia,' up spake an old musician, 'Sir,' he said, 'if Mozart had heard you he would have grasped your hand and cried " Bravo ! "

An insignificant old man like myself dare not do so.' Chopin then played a Mazurka as a farewell, and no sooner had he finished than the postmaster, taking him up in his arms, carried him bodily to the coach. But the most amusing part of the whole scene is yet to come, for the postillion, still suffering under the anathematisation of his master, and jealous because the pretty servant girl, to whom he was doubtless attached, could not take her eyes off the young musician, whispered in her ear, 'Things do go unfairly in this world. The young gentleman is carried into the coach by the master himself; the like of us must climb laboriously on the box unassisted, though we are *musical.*'

It will be noticed that in most of the anecdotes relating to Chopin's playing, that he is invariably spoken of as having 'improvised,' and there is a story told of how, when playing the organ at service in the Wizytck Church, he became so absorbed in his extemporisation as to be entirely oblivious to his surroundings, and, heeding neither priest nor congregation, did not cease until a considerable portion of the service had been gone through. But however doubtful we may be of the veracity of this pretty story (and there are many things which point to exaggeration in it) we nevertheless have good reason to believe that Chopin's indulgence in the art of simultaneous creation and exposition was great. And he seems to have carried it even further, for many of his compositions could fitly be called only 'improvisations with the pen.' Moreover, we venture to believe that the excessive indulgence in this charming, though dangerous, relaxation has much to answer for as regards a great deal that is unsatisfactory in his works, for we know that many of them were composed at the piano. Now, let us see what Schumann says about this :—' Above all things, persist in composing mentally, *without the aid of the instrument* [the italics are ours]. Turn over your melodic ideas in your head until you can say to yourself "It is well done."' Again he says, ' If you can pick out melodies at the piano you will be pleased; but if they come to you spontaneously away from the piano, you will have still more reason to be delighted, for then the inner tone-sense is roused to activity. The fingers must do what the head wishes, and not *vice versâ.*' Now Schumann, on this subject, carries especial weight, for up to the year 1839 he composed exclusively at the instrument, while after that time he discarded it entirely. Moreover, if we take the masterpieces of the greatest musicians, we shall find that the greatest ideas contained in them were invariably conceived while in the open air, and not only conceived, but frequently elaborated and finished without the smallest aid from the instrument.

Now, with regard to Chopin, George Sand tells us that his creativeness 'descended upon his piano suddenly, completely, sublimely, or it sang itself in his head during his walks, and he made haste to hear it by rushing to the instrument.' Therefore we may safely assume that Chopin composed in both ways; but judging from the works themselves there is a greater number bearing the impress of improvisation than that of musical thought. We cannot conscientiously call Chopin a great musical thinker. We do not for one moment intend to convey that his ideas were derived from the instrument, but what we do mean is, that those effects which were essentially of the piano should not have been used to such excess as to in any way mar the pure musical thought.   And this is frequently what does happen. That very harmonic luxuriance at times so jades our senses that we involuntarily gasp for a purer air. But if we look closely into the melodic material, we often find that it is in no way unsuitable to 'crisper' harmonic treatment, and that the composition, as a whole, would often be the gainer thereby.   In fact, what Chopin too often denies us is contrast in the colouring of his themes. He frequently varies the detail, but nevertheless allows the tone-colour to remain unaltered. Those extended harmonies are doubtless in themselves most beautiful, but how much more beautiful is their effect when contrasted with closely-knit chords ? Of course we must not lose sight of the fact, that he has in the pianoforte no such scope for effect and change of colour as is afforded the musician who uses the orchestra as a means for his expression ; nor when we consider this do we under-estimate the genius of the man in obtaining from a percussion instrument the many wonderful effects which he undoubtedly does. Moreover, it may be argued that the emotions he wished to express demanded the treatment to which he subjected his material, and that the harmonic conception was simultaneous with the melodic. But if in some cases that be so, the works must in parts be false, inasmuch as their æsthetic effect is at times incongruous. That he was true to his own emotional schedule we know, nor would we have him otherwise, but we do say that there are times when he is melodically joyful, or at least does his best to be so. And then it is that, by the indiscriminate use, or rather abuse, of such particularities as we have instanced, they cease for the time to be artistic, and degenerate into nothing more nor less than mannerisms. It can never be said of Chopin that his imagination cowered before his culture, as it frequently did and does with some musicians. Such a thing would have been at total variance with his theories. All that we wish to show is, that personality in composition, when fostered by artificial means, such as is the pianoforte, will, even in the case of composition for that instrument, degenerate into mannerism if not carefully guarded. The temptation, especially to a pianist like Chopin, must have been great, for did not Schumann—who was in no wise such a master of the instrument as Chopin—say of the *Davidstänze,* which he had composed at the piano, 'If ever I was happy at the piano it was when I composed those pieces.' Chopin was of course but human, and such scenes as that which took place at Züllichau doubtless did much to increase his love for improvisation ; indeed, we are told that in after life he valued the appreciation of those plain folks far more than the adulation which was showered upon him by the artistic aristocracy of the French capital. This we can easily believe, inasmuch as a true artist loves sincerity either in his art or in the appreciation of it.

But we have strayed somewhat from our course, and haste to chronicle the composer's return to Warsaw, where he arrived safely on the 6th October. His time at home, however, was to be limited to a few months, for in the following year he undertook a journey which was considerably more extensive and eventful than the short visit he had just paid to Berlin. From this time forth, the young man, parted from his family, naturally gathers around him kindred spirits, whom we designate by the name of friends. Some of these friendships were formed while at the Lyceum, others were the result of his travels. But as the names of several of his Polish friends will continually crop up in connection with his letters and otherwise, we shall here briefly refer to them. First and foremost was Titus Woyciechowski, who had been his school companion, and who lived on his family estate in Poland, and the long friendship with whom was only severed by death. To him are most of Chopin's letters, outside of his family, addressed. Next to him in point of intimacy was John Matuszynski, a young medical student of Warsaw, to whom also several of his letters are written. Under the head of companions with whom there did not exist the same amount of intimacy were Celinski, Hube, and Maciejowski, who, as we shall see in the next chapter, accompanied Chopin on his travels. Also amongst his musical acquaintances at this time we have the names of Julius Fontana, who was a daily visitor at Chopin's house; Joseph Nowakowski, Thomas Nidecki, and Felix Dobrzynski, the last-named having been a fellow-student with Chopin under Elsner.

There remains now little of interest in connection with our young artist, until we can follow him on his next journey, which we propose to do in the next chapter. We will, therefore, take for consideration here some of the works which followed those noticed in the last chapter.

The Op. 4, which is the next in order, was a Sonata for the pianoforte in C minor. Although it was published posthumously, we shall consider it as belonging to the group of 'Sonatas,' inasmuch as it remained in MS. through the fault of the publisher and not of Chopin, who sent it for publication in 1828, and it therefore is, to all intents and purposes, to be regarded in the same light as its companions. The Op. 5 is entitled *Rondeau à la Mazur*, and is in F major. It is dedicated to the Countess de Moriolles, and although it exhibits more evidence of the development of his style, it cannot be considered as an important work. We therefore pass on to the Mazurkas.

Opera 6 and 7 we find to contain respectively four and five examples of this form of composition, besides which there were published during the composer's lifetime thirty-two others. It will be most convenient, then, to glance at the whole group. First, as to the Mazurka itself. The Mazurka or Mazurek, as it is also called, is one of the chief dances of Poland, and one which Chopin specially loved. It had its origin in Mazovia, and has in its turn formed the basis of many of the late Polish dances. While the time is the same ($\frac{3}{8}$ or $\frac{3}{4}$) the movement of the dance is somewhat slower than that of the waltz; while the rhythm is totally different, being as follows;—

but in this respect Chopin invariably departs from the original, and subjects his rhythm to much variety of development. For instance, he frequently employs such variations of it as the following :—

or this:—

and thereby relieves any monotony which might arise from constant adherence to the original, at the same time preserving the whole spirit of the form. The

Mazurka was originally essentially a dance of the Polish peasantry, but was later adopted to a very great extent by the aristocracy of the country. It resembles not a little the French quadrille, and forms an exception to most dances, for in it the male sex is enabled to appear to great advantage, for, says a Polish writer (Brodzinski)[1]: 'A young man, and more especially a young Pole, remarkable for a certain amiable boldness, soon becomes the soul and hero of this dance.' We can readily conceive this to be the case, especially as the men invariably wear military uniform. 'The female dancer' (to quote from the same authority), 'lightly dressed, scarcely skimming the earth with her dainty foot, holding on by the hand of her partner, in the twinkling of an eye carried away by several others, and then like lightning per-cipitating herself again into the arms of the first, offers the image of the most happy and delightful creature.'

The music is of course purely national, and we English are therefore under a decided disadvantage as regards the full comprehension of such compositions as these Mazurkas. The same applies to the Polon-

---

[1] Niecks's *Life of Chopin.*

aises. The qualities of Chopin's muse in these works are such as appeal most directly to his fellow-countrymen. For instance, it is difficult for us to sympathise with the Poles in their partiality to dancing to tunes in minor keys, but here it is perhaps that they illustrate very forcibly their proverb which says, 'A fig for misery.' Nevertheless, there is in these products of Chopin's genius much that is of interest to the musician. In some cases he so revels in his luxuriance of national melody as to throw all else to the winds, and to write progressions which would drive the purist in musical grammar on the border of distraction. Thus it is, then, that 'these Mazurkas lose half their meaning if played without a certain freedom and license—impossible to imitate, but irresistible if the player at all feels the music.' This was the opinion of Mr. Chorley, critic of the *Athenæum*, who heard Chopin play them in London. There is, of course, to be found in all the Mazurkas a strong family likeness, yet while they all so resemble one another, the harmonic and rhythmic ideas are so varied as to make no two exactly alike. It would be impossible, on account of their number, to consider here the many striking features of these fantastic miniatures, and to do them justice. We must therefore content ourselves with having glanced at a few of their prevailing characteristics.

Nevertheless, we cannot leave them without noting a technical detail, which is especially noticeable in these and many other of the works. That is the frequent use by Chopin of a sequence of the chords of the seventh. The following is a prominent example of this.

Vide Op. 17, No. 1.

The next composition which claims our attention is the Op. 8, Trio for pianoforte, violin, and violoncello, in G minor. This we regard as one of the most perfect, and, unfortunately, most neglected of Chopin's works. It is in sonata form, and has the four movements, Allegro, Scherzo, Adagio, and finale. The work opens with a short preamble of eight bars, in the last of which the principal theme is announced by the violin, the pianoforte accompanying with arpeggio chords until the tenth bar is reached, when it takes up the theme in octaves. We then have a tributary with the following beautiful pianoforte figure, of which the

inner part is doubled by the violin, and the bass by the 'cello. This continues until we come to an episode, also in G minor, for the string instrument, the pianoforte accompaniment consisting of short chords, accentuating the rhythm; this also comes to a close in G minor. And here we may mention that this pre-valence of the tonic key seems to us the only blot to mar the movement. By-and-by we get a short digression into the key of E flat, but we no sooner begin to feel the benefit of it than we are led back again to the inevitable primary key. The 'Scherzo'

is delightful, and the movement so flowing and full of
life that it carries us along irresistibly, while it is
difficult in the domain of chamber music to name a
more beautiful movement than the Adagio. Here is
the lovely theme first announced by the pianoforte :—

and taken up by the violin, and we can quite understand the admiration which the work aroused in
Schumann, when he described it as being ' as noble
as possible, more full of enthusiasm than the work
of any other tone poet, original in its most minute
details, and every note music and life.'

CHAPTER IV

Chopin's next journey was to Vienna. In July 1829 we find him starting for the Austrian capital, in company with his friends Maciejowski, Hube, and Celinski. The party stopped a week on the way at Cracow, the ancient Polish capital, exploring the town and neighbourhood, which presented many features of interest to the lover of Poland and things Polish. Having made this pleasurable halt, they continued their journey to Vienna, arriving in that city on or about the last day of July. Chopin had brought with him, amongst others, a letter of introduction from Elsner to Haslinger, the music publisher at Vienna, and one of the first things he did after arrival was to present it. He had already sent Haslinger some manuscripts, which the publisher had promised to bring out, but which, nevertheless, still remained in MS. He describes his

reception by Haslinger as being most cordial, the
publisher promising him that his ‘Variations’ should
shortly appear in a musical periodical, entitled the
Odeon, which he was bringing out. At the same
time he strongly advised Chopin to let the public
hear him play, but experienced considerable difficulty
in overcoming the young artist’s prejudice against
so doing. It is probable that Chopin felt some mis-
givings about playing in the city which had heard
Beethoven and Mozart, and, moreover, he realised
that it was a widely different thing to playing before
his own countrymen and in his own country, where
records of his wonderful performances had widely
gone forth. There seems to have been no lack of
interest brought to bear upon him with the object
of inducing him to give a concert. Count Gallenberg,
the lessee of the Kärnthnerthor Theatre at the
time, even went so far as to place the house at
his disposal for the purpose, and was backed up
heartily by his *capellmeister*, Würfel, and Blahetka,
a journalist well known and of some influence, both
of whom assured Chopin of their belief in his success.
At length he was overcome by their arguments, and

the concert duly announced, and on 11th August Chopin made his first bow to the Viennese public. The programme included Beethoven's Overture to Prometheus, the Don Juan Variations, the Krakowiak Rondo, an aria of Rossini and one of Vaccaj's sung by Mdlle. Veltheim; besides which Chopin gave them a short improvisation. Writing of the concert to Woyciechowski, he says: 'This first appearance before the Viennese public did not in the least excite me, and I sat down to play on a splendid instrument of Graff's, perhaps the best in Vienna. A painted young man, who prided himself upon having performed the same service for Moscheles, Hummel, and Herz, turned over the leaves for me in the Variations. Notwithstanding that I was in a desperate mood the Variations pleased so much that I was recalled several times. Mdlle. Veltheim sang exquisitely, and my improvisation was followed by much applause and many recalls.' The press was as unanimous as the public in his praise, and the concert would have been an unqualified success had it not been for some slight disagreeableness on the part of the members of the orchestra. We can best get an idea of this from his letter:—'The members of the orchestra were evidently annoyed with me at rehearsal: I think what vexed them most was my desire to make my *début* with a new composition. I commenced with the Variations, which were in their turn to be followed by the Rondo Krakowiak. We got through the Variations well enough, but the Rondo went so badly that we had to begin twice from the commencement; this appears to have been caused by my bad writing. I ought to have placed the figures above instead of below the rests, as that appears to be the method to which the Viennese musicians are accustomed.'

Apart from this, the only criticism at all adverse seems to have been on the part of one or two who pronounced Chopin's playing to err on the side of softness and delicacy, but, as he himself said, that was only because they were 'accustomed to the drum-beating of their own virtuosi.'

He was peculiarly sensible to anything in the way of adverse newspaper criticism, for on one occasion he wrote:—'If the newspapers cut me up so much that I shall not venture before the world again, I have resolved to become a house-painter; that would be as easy as anything else, and I should, at all events, still be an artist.'

On August the 20th Chopin gave his second concert in Vienna, and seems to have set the seal upon the success which he had already achieved, but he writes:—'Under no circumstances will I give a third concert; I only give this second one because I am forced to, for I thought that people in Warsaw might say, "He only gave one concert in Vienna, so he could not have been much liked."'

At the second concert the 'Variations' were, by special request, repeated, and the Rondo which, although in the programme of the first concert, had been omitted, was on this occasion produced. Speaking of it as a composition, one of the chief Vienna critics said that, 'while the piece rarely rose to geniality, it nevertheless had passages which were distinguished by careful and thoughtful workmanship, though, on the whole, it lacked variety. Of his playing there was but slight qualification of the praise bestowed; for the same critic wrote:—'The master showed his dexterity as a pianist to perfection, and

E

overcame with seemingly small trouble the greatest difficulties, and connoisseurs and amateurs alike manifested loudly their recognition of his wonderful playing.' He spent only three weeks in Vienna, yet in that short time he managed to do a good deal. He took the opportunity of being present at the performances of Rossini's *Cenerentola*, Boieldieu's *Dame Blanche*, and Meyerbeer's *Crociato in Egitto*, besides which he established the most friendly relations with Czerny, Haslinger, Lachner, Kreutzer, and others. His popularity increased as he was known, and astonished him, for he said, ' people wonder at me so, that I positively wonder at them for wondering at me.' Indeed, his reception was enthusiastic in the extreme, and the parting was regretted on all sides. Miss Blahetka (whose father had been partly instrumental in inducing Chopin to give his first concert), and who was herself a pianist and composer, presented Chopin with a copy of her compositions bearing her signature, as a memento of his visit; and the many artists whose acquaintance Chopin had made in Vienna met together in order to say farewell, and give the young artist a happy send-off, one and all begging him to return soon.

Prague was now their destination, and in the Bohemian city they arrived on August 21. Whilst in Vienna, Würfel and Blahetka had provided Chopin with letters of introduction to all the musical celebrities in Prague, chief amongst whom at this time was Frederick Pixis, professor of the violin at the Conservatoire, and conductor at the theatre. At the house of Pixis he was fortunate enough to meet Alex. Klengel of Dresden, who happened to be passing through Prague on his way to Vienna. Klengel played his fugues to Chopin, who, in a letter, expresses himself as pleased with the great contrapuntist, although, he was obliged to confess, somewhat disappointed with his performance. Pressed to stay and give a concert, he refused, mindful, no doubt, of the very severe manner in which Paganini, the violinist, had, on the occasion of his appearance there, been handled by the critics of Prague. So after pleasantly spending three days in the capital of Bohemia, they pursued their way *via* Teplitz to Dresden, which latter place they reached on the 26th August.

His visit to this city was uneventful, for beyond witnessing a performance of *Faust*, with Charles

Devrient (nephew of the great Louis Devrient) in the title-rôle, and paying a visit to the Capellmeister Morlacchi, there is absolutely nothing of interest chronicled of his short stay. The remainder of the journey to Warsaw was made by way of Breslau, and we find Chopin once again installed in his native city in the early part of September.

But the taste he had just had of the world, and more especially of the artistic world, had its effect upon Chopin, and he found it impossible to settle down in Warsaw, and work steadily on as he had done before he left it. Moreover, such a course was rendered the more impossible, owing to his having become the victim of a passion, perhaps as intense as it was short-lived, for the opera-singer Constantia Gladkowska. While writing to his friend Titus, and stating that 'in no case would he remain the winter in Warsaw,' he goes on to say, 'do not think for one moment that, when I urge the advantages of a stay in Vienna, I am thinking of Miss Blahetka, of whom I have already written to you. for I have—perhaps to my misfortune—already found my ideal, which I worship faithfully and sincerely. Six months have now passed, and I have not yet exchanged a word with her of whom I nightly dream. Whilst thinking of her I composed the Adagio of my Concerto,[1] and early this morning she inspired the waltz,[1] which I send you with this letter.' Concerning this episode in Chopin's life we have from Liszt a description which, in a manner thoroughly characteristic of him, he surrounds with a halo of sentiment and mystery grossly exaggerated. This is what he tells:—'The tempest, which in one of its sudden gusts tore Chopin from his native soil, like a bird dreamy and abstracted, surprised by the storm upon the branches of a foreign tree, sundered the ties of this first love, and robbed the exile of a faithful and devoted wife, as well as disinherited him of a country.' The young girl, he adds, was sweet and beautiful. Chopin like a 'dreamy and abstracted bird upon a foreign tree' surely savours rather of the ridiculous!

We know that, although of no very long duration, Chopin's attachment for this young singer was serious

---

[1] The Concerto in F minor, and the Waltz, Op. 70, in D flat.

while it lasted; of this it is not difficult to judge from
a letter written some time later from Vienna, in which
he says:—'God forbid that she should suffer in any
way on my account. Let her mind be at rest, and
tell her that so long as my heart beats I shall not
cease to adore her. Tell her, that even after death,
my ashes shall be strewn beneath her feet.' And
much more in the same strain. Neither must we
lose sight of the fact that she was quite a girl,
and at the time engaged in studying vocalisa-
tion at the Conservatoire. To Chopin, therefore,
was such an event as her *début* upon the operatic
stage, which occurred about this time, doubly interesting, and we can forgive him for launching
forth in praise of his divinity as he did upon the
occasion, especially as she was in no wise a bad
singer. Chopin was, therefore, as we have said, very
restless in his native town; indeed he himself wrote:
—'If I were not so happy in my home circle, I
should certainly not live here.' He was continually
forming plans for going abroad, and inclined, above
all, to return to Vienna, although his father wished
him to go to Berlin, in which city Prince Radziwill and

his wife had invited the young musician to stay with them. This invitation Chopin did not accept, although he did accept that of the prince to visit him at Antonin, his country seat. Thither he set out in October, and seems to have passed a very pleasant time with the prince and his family, and indeed, not to have been blind to the fascinations of the prince's charming daughters, one of whom was an excellent pianiste. The prince himself was no mean performer on the violoncello, and he and Chopin played a good deal together. Writing from Antonin, Chopin says:—'I have written during my stay here an *Alla Polacca* with violoncello. It is nothing more than a brilliant salon piece, such as pleases ladies. I should like the Princess Wanda to practise it. She is only seventeen years of age, and very béautiful; it would be delightful to have the pleasure of placing her pretty fingers upon the keys.' I think this sentence sufficiently demonstrates that Chopin was not so absolutely engrossed with his love for Constantia Gladkowska as to be oblivious to all else. With him it was invariably 'out of sight out of mind,' and he was ever a victim to the latest impression.

With the additional attraction of having a musician in his host, it may be easily imagined that Chopin was loth to leave such charming society; but he felt that it was incumbent upon him to get on with his composition, and the F minor Concerto still lacked a 'finale.'

At this time he also composed some studies, most of the Op. 10, which we shall shortly proceed to discuss. But before doing so it is necessary to notice the concerts given at this time by Chopin in Warsaw. The first of these took place on March 17, 1830, and the programme included such pieces as the overture to *Leszek Bialy* from an opera by Elsner, Allegro from the Concerto in F minor, and Adagio and Rondo from the same Concerto, some Variations by Paër, sung by Madame Meier and a pot-pourri on national airs, composed and played by Chopin. Of these the Adagio and Rondo proved most successful; but still the old complaint was made against him, namely, want of power.

The full beauty and 'finesse' of Chopin's playing was never really fully understood by his own countrymen in Warsaw. He appealed to them most when, as in the Krakowiak or Fantasia, he gave them the bare national material more or less furbished and elaborated by himself. Of his finer and more original efforts they showed nothing like the same appreciation. The second concert followed a week later. In the programme we find a symphony by Nowakowski, the Rondo Krakowiak, an aria from *Elena e Malvina*, by Soliva, sung by Mme. Meier, and again two movements from the F minor concerto. He also improvised on Polish national airs. The press was most eulogistic, and congratulations poured in upon him from all sides, and although he did not seem to think anything of the financial result, he had, nevertheless, every reason to be thankful, for the net proceeds from both concerts came out at something over £100. He had made up his mind to give a third concert, but deemed it best to postpone doing so until within a short time of his departure. This, as it turned out, was further off than he anticipated. In the meantime he continued to make progress with his composition, and while at work on a new concerto still found time for the completion of several *Etudes*, which it will be convenient here to consider ; although, of course, many of the collection were not written until later. The title 'studies' has generally been understood to mean pieces written without necessarily any musical inspiration, and having solely for their object the practice or perfection of any mechanical difficulty. This cannot be said to be wholly the case with the *Etudes* of Chopin. They were undoubtedly written with a view to the further development of the technique, and are, when looked at from that point of view, perfect. But at the same time their æsthetic value is as great as that of any of his works. It is evident that nothing but the greatest 'finesse' in pianoforte playing satisfied Chopin; above all, he valued in a pupil a delicate and sympathetic touch. This he very rarely found, consequently its cultivation was invariably the first thing towards which he directed his attention in a pupil.

Hitherto the methods of Emanuel Bach and Clementi had been generally accepted as all that was needful for the playing of any composition then written for the pianoforte. And this was so, generally speaking. For the features of modern pianoforte playing for which it is found to be inadequate, are the work of such romanticists as Chopin, Schumann, and Liszt. With them an entirely new horizon in the art of piano playing was opened up. The whole characteristic of our modern pianoforte school is the result of romanticism and not of classicism. For while classicism is the perfection of form, romanticism does not hesitate to express the individuality and personality of the composer, even so far as writing music, which may seem certainly untuneful, if not harsh, to the ear, should the thoughts and intention of the composer be such. And certainly our thoughts and emotions change in seconds rather than in minutes. When, therefore, the emotional and romantic works of such men as Schumann and Chopin were created, the old school of pianoforte technique was quite inadequate as a means of their æsthetic expression. There is no doubt that a great deal of the difficulty at first experienced in the rendering of Schumann's pianoforte works was owing to defects in the pianoforte technique of their composer; but this was not the case with Chopin, who, as we know, had been thoroughly trained in the art of pianoforte playing.

and was familiar with, and master of, all the resources of the instrument. Another great difficulty
encountered in Schumann's music lay in the complicated rhythms, and the use of both hands in the
playing of one musical phrase. And here, again,
Chopin differs from him, for no matter to what extent he may wish the *tempo rubato* used, it is rarely
indulged in but by one of the hands, the other
invariably marking a clear beat. Chopin also introduced absolutely new methods of fingering, and
entirely threw over such accepted *dicta* as, for
instance, 'the thumb or fourth finger should never
be used on the black keys except in very rare cases.'
The quality which he valued most in the player was a
sympathetic touch, and for the attainment of this he
maintained the first requisite to be an easy position
of the hand. To this matter he gave much care and
thought,—with this conclusion, that in order to
obtain at once a graceful and commanding position, the hands should be placed so that the five
fingers of the right hand rested on the notes E,
F sharp, G sharp, A sharp, and B, and those of the
left on C, B flat, G flat, and F flat. If the fingers
are placed upon these notes of the instrument,

it will be found that the hands are somewhat
turned in opposite directions, and are more ready
for the rapid execution of scale passages and *arpeggi*
than in any other position. When teaching a pupil
Chopin adhered strictly to this, and would even for
the while submit to the uneven execution of some
passages, until the pupil became used to his position
of the hands. Chopin it was who initiated pianoforte
players in the matter of having the second and third
fingers over the fourth in ascending passages, while
he frequently passed the thumb after the third or
fourth finger. All such movements had, of course,
to be played until they were got so smoothly
that the shifting of the fingers was in no way noticeable. As a result of such innovations as these, it
became necessary that studies should be written
which should, by bringing in these new features,
render the execution of them perfect. These we
shall now proceed to notice severally. We find them
under Op. Nos. 10 and 25, entitled respectively
Twelve Grand Studies, and Twelve Studies, besides
which we have Three New Studies on the 'Méthode
des Méthodes,' of Moscheles and Fetis, without Opus
number, but which were published about 1840. Of

the first group, Op. 10, we will first notice No. 2, which is particularly illustrative of Chopin's method of passing the second and third fingers over the fourth, to which we have just alluded.

Perhaps if we might single out any particular one as being more beautiful than its companions, it would be No. 3 of this group. The movement is *Lento ma non Troppo*, and there is one long chain of entrancing melody and harmony throughout. What could be more expressive of tender ' longing ' than the following phrase of four bars, which occurs at the eighteenth bar.

Chopin himself considered this study to contain

the most bautiful melody he ever wrote, but it
would be at once difficult and invidious to make
a selection amid such a casket of gems. We
would fain linger over these studies, but must be
content with picking out those which are especially
conspicuous, either from an æsthetic point of view or
by their purpose, that is, the development of some
technical difficulty. Midway between this classifica-
tion may be said to come No. 5, which, although
having for its object the perfecting of the technique
(the right hand playing only the black notes), has
such an amount of brilliancy as to raise it to a higher
level, though it is not to be compared to the poetical
No. 3, for instance. The colour of No. 6 is sombre in
the extreme. The accompanying semi-quaver is
treated chromatically throughout, the bass being firm
and dignified. Notice the peculiar 'Major' effect of
the last bar but 4, when we are interrupted by

which comes upon us like the sun emerging from a mass of dark clouds, only once more to disappear from our view, and leave us in our former half-light. In No. 7 of the same set there is nothing calling for special notice. It is not nearly so Chopinesque as its companions; indeed, in the fourth and fifth bars of this study we find a distinct Mendelssohnian flavour. Curiously enough, in the following No. 9 we again come upon a similarity of idea with Mendelssohn. Compare this *Etude* in F minor with Mendelssohn's *Lied Ohne Worte*, No. 6 in F sharp minor. The 'germ' of the idea is certainly very similar, though the development of it differs entirely, the one being an *andante tranquillo*, and the other being marked *allegro molto agitato*. No. 11 is interesting as a study in the extended harmonies so often met with in the other compositions. On opening the Op. 25 we are immediately struck by the great clearness of the melody of the first number. It is more sequential and straightforward than usual; one might almost compare it to a beautiful fabric from which the pattern stands out boldly, while the weaving of the texture beneath is of the finest. There is

nothing in the least approaching the 'morbid' in it,
which is the more noticeable, as it is in that direction that we must look to account for much that is
unsatisfactory in the children of Chopin's genius.
No. 6 is evidently written as an exercise for the clear
and even execution of 'thirds.' In No. 7, again, we
find an example of the composer's great wealth of
melody. The key is C sharp minor, and the first bars
are unutterably sad, but here we cannot agree with
Professor Niecks, who finds the work monotonous; on
the contrary, it is, to our mind, one of the most beautiful of them all. Notice in this work the elaborate
cadenzas for the left hand, the right hand acting as
conductor and keeping the rhythm. No. 8 is a study
in 'sixths' for the right hand, No. 10 a study in
octaves for the left hand. Had Professor Niecks
applied the term monotonous to No. 12, we should
have been more ready to endorse his opinion, as,
although great power is manifested, the very 'same-
ness' of the form of the *arpeggio* figure causes a
certain amount of monotony to be felt. Of the
Three New Studies, No. 3 is a little gem. The
melodic grace is charming, and seems to flow from an

endless stream. It is interesting here to notice little evidences of 'personality,' perhaps almost mannerisms, which go to show that the same hand which wrote this study also penned the Scherzo in B flat minor, Op. 31. With this we come to the end of the *Etudes*. It is only when we are intimate with these truly pathetic utterances that we recognise the insufficiency of the technical name applied to them. They can only compare with the preludes (also a misapplied title) as being expressive of Chopin's most personal feelings, and what we may term the ' dreamy ' side of his genius.

CHAPTER V

'WARSAW, *Sep.* 18*th*, 1830.

'I do not quite know why I am still here, but I am happy, and my parents agree to my remaining. Last Wednesday I tried my concerto with quartet accompaniment, but cannot say that I was altogether satisfied with it. Those who were present at the rehearsal say that the finale is the most successful movement—perhaps because it is the one easiest understood. I shall not be able to tell you until next week how it will sound with the full orchestra. . . . To-morrow I am to have another rehearsal with the quartet, and then I shall go—whither? I have no special attraction anywhere, but, in any event, I shall not remain in Warsaw. If you think that it is some beloved object that keeps me here, you are wrong, like a good many other people. I can assure you that, so far as I myself am concerned, I am ready for any sacrifice. I love, but I must keep my unhappy passion locked in my own breast for some years longer . . . I was at great big C.'s yesterday, for his name-day, when I took part in Spohr's Quintet for piano, clarinet, bassoon, French horn, and flute. The work is extremely beautiful, but I do not find the pianoforte part very playable. . . . Instead of commencing at seven o'clock we did not begin until eleven. You are doubtless surprised that I was not fast asleep. But there was a very good reason why I should keep awake, for among the guests was a very beautiful girl, who vividly reminded me of my ideal; just fancy, I stayed till three A.M. I intended to have started for Vienna this day week, but finally gave up the idea—perhaps you can guess why. You may rest assured that I am no egoist, and as truly as I love you I would make any sacrifice for other people; but not for outside appearances; for public opinion, which is much valued here, although I am not influenced by it, regards it as a calamity for one to have a shabby coat or hat. If I fail in my profession, and wake up some morning to find myself without anything to eat, you must get a clerkship for me at Poturzya. I shall be quite as happy in a stable as I was in your castle last summer. So long as I have health and strength I will gladly work all my days. . . . People often lose the good opinion of others by trying to gain it; but I do not think that I shall either raise or lower myself in your estimation by singing my own praises, for I feel there is mutual sympathy between us.'

We have quoted somewhat lengthily from this letter, chiefly because it is so very typical of his character. There is in it so much of that indecision, that want of strength of mind, which so influenced the whole of Chopin's life. Notice how, after expressing the great depth of his love for his ideal, and volunteering to make any sacrifice for her, he is quite willing for the time being to accept the shadow for the substance, and amuse himself heartily with the pretty young lady who reminded him of his 'ideal.' Again, mark his great indecision with regard to his movements. First he decides he will go, then he changes his mind, and so on. This was always so with Chopin. He resigned himself to whatever influence happened to be the latest and the strongest.

It was often in his mind to do the wisest and the kindest things; but how often did he do them? and simply because he allowed himself to be swept away by others who were more strong-willed than himself. We may doubtless assume that much of this weakness of character was due to the lack of stamina in his constitution, but apart from that it was his prevailing characteristic, and shows itself at times most forcibly in his art.

The third concert given by Chopin in Warsaw ultimately took place on 11th October 1830. He had in the meantime completed the E minor Concerto, which formed the chief feature of the programme. Besides this were given a symphony by Görner, the overture to Rossini's *William Tell*, the Cavatina from the same master's *La Donna del Lago*, sung by Miss Gladkowska, and Fantasia on the Polish airs. The success of the concert was complete, Chopin excelling himself in the Concerto, which, having had the advantage of much rehearsal, benefited accordingly. Especially successful also was the Fantasia, while Chopin himself was greatly delighted with the masterly way in which Soliva conducted the performance. Altogether this was one of the most successful concerts he ever gave.

On the 1st November Chopin took his departure once again for Vienna, Elsner and several of his friends accompanying him as far as Wola, the first village beyond Warsaw. Here they were met by the pupils of the Conservatoire, who sang a Cantata, which had been composed by Elsner for the occasion. Having taken leave of his friends and family, Chopin proceeded on his journey, and at Kalisz was joined by his *fidus Achates*, Titus Woyciechowski, after which they travelled together to Vienna by way of Breslau. Here they halted for a time, Chopin taking the opportunity of renewing his acquaintance with the Capellmeister Schnabel. The latter invited Chopin to accompany him to rehearsal one morning. On this occasion the Concerto in E flat of Moscheles was about to be rehearsed, and the pianoforte solo was to be played by a young amateur. On the appearance of Chopin the young fellow began to display evident signs of nervousness, and begged to be excused his part of the performance. Consequently, on being pressed to play in his stead, our artist consented, and driving straightway back to his hotel, got his music, and returned to rehearse the E minor Concerto, which was given the same evening. He seems to have considerably astonished everybody; indeed, they were quite at a loss what to make of him, yet no one thought of denying that they were in the presence, and under the spell, of a great artist.

Leaving Breslau on 10th November, his next place of call was Dresden, where he arrived two days later. In this city he made several friends, amongst whom must be mentioned Vincent Rastrelli, and Rolla the violinist, whilst he had the opportunity of cementing the friendship already formed with Klengel. His intention at this time was to proceed finally from Vienna to Milan, and, knowing this, Rubini (a brother of the celebrated tenor) and Rolla provided him with letters to the most influential people in the musical world of Northern Italy. But, as we shall see, this project was not destined to be carried out. Passing through Prague, Vienna was reached at the end of November. Here they put up at a hotel until the apartments which they had taken were vacant, and they were enabled to take possession of them. At his reception in Vienna we fear Chopin was somewhat disappointed. The success he had made there had led him to expect an enthusiastic reception from such people as publishers and managers on his return; and, as is frequently the case with people of his enthusiastic and artistic temperament, he imagined that everyone was so interested in his success that it was a matter of as much moment to them as to him. But although he had undoubtedly pleased greatly at the time of his former visit, he was very soon forgotten, and his success merged in that of other artists who had later occupied the public attention. His sense of disappointment was in no degree lessened by the result of his visit to Haslinger, who, it will be remembered, still had the ms. of his Don Juan 'Variations.' The publisher absolutely declined to print this work; neither could he be persuaded to have anything to do with the F minor Concerto. Haslinger had been assured — if such assurance he needed — of the excellence of Chopin's work; more than this, he had proof of its success with the public. Yet he would have none of it. No doubt the business man will

say: 'It is not to be expected that a publisher will print works which, for some reason or other of his own, he considers unlikely to sell.' Nevertheless, if a publisher is content to make handsome profits out of the lighter forms of a composer's art, it is only right that he should benefit art, and the composer, by publishing those works which, although they may not be the direct means of filling his coffers, can, nevertheless, reflect nothing but credit on all concerned in their production. But Haslinger was pig-headed, and stuck to his opinion, and the Variations and Concerto remained for the present in their MS. state. Count Gallenberg, who had so assisted Chopin on his former visit, had been obliged, owing to heavy financial losses, to relinquish his contract and retire from the management of the theatre. To the new manager, Duport, Chopin was introduced by Hummel. But the results were not satisfactory. Duport would guarantee nothing, and did not encourage him to give a concert at all. So that it is small wonder that we find Chopin writing to Elsner in a tone nothing short of despondent. Says he:—
'I meet with obstacles on every side. Not only does a

series of wretched pianoforte concerts entirely ruin all real music and tire the public, but the occurrences in Poland have also had their effect upon my position.'

To add to his other troubles, the insurrection in Poland—which is the occurrence to which he alludes — caused the return to that country of his friend Titus. This left poor Chopin quite heart-broken, and so desperately did he feel his loneliness that in one of his weaker moments he actually took post-horses and attempted to overtake his friend; but finding it useless he returned to Vienna. Such actions as these serve to show us how hopelessly incap-able he was of withstanding the ordinary trials and troubles of life, especially of an artist's life, which is of all, perhaps, the most beset with them. Discouraged on all sides, he at length abandoned all idea of concert giving in Vienna, and so little able did he feel himself to cope with the life he had entered upon, that he wrote to Matuszynski: 'I would not willingly be a burden to my father; were I not in fear of that I should at once return to Warsaw. I often feel that I curse the moment in which I ever left my home. You will, I am sure, feel for me in my condition, and understand that since Titus went away too much has suddenly fallen upon me. The numerous dinners, soirées, concerts, and balls, which I am obliged to be present at, only weary me. I am very melancholy, and feel so lonely and deserted here. There is no soul in whom I can unreservedly confide, yet I have so many "friends"——'

His indecision and weakness of character shows up very conspicuously under these trials, and he seems only able to lean on his parents and friends for advice as to what would be best for him to do. 'I do not know,' he says, 'whether I ought to go soon to Italy or wait a little longer. Please, dearest father, let me know your and my good mother's wish in this matter,' and again he asks his friend Matuszynski, 'Shall I return home? Shall I stay here? Shall I kill myself? or shall I go to Paris?' Fate decided for him in so far as going to Italy was concerned, for the political disturbances then taking place in that country rendered a visit there at the time quite out of the question. But even when he had made up his mind that it would be best for him to go to Paris, there still remained the weighty question as to when he should put his decision into execution. In the meantime he pursued a very quiet life in Vienna ; of this we can get no better idea than from one of his letters. Thus he writes:—'The intolerably stupid servant calls me early, and I rise, take my coffee, which is frequently quite cold, owing to my forgetting my breakfast for my music. My German teacher appears punctually at nine o'clock, after which I generally write. Hummel (son of the composer) comes to work at my portrait, and Nidecki to study my concerto. I remain in my comfortable dressing-gown until twelve o'clock, at which hour Dr. Liebenfrost, a lawyer, sometimes drops in to see me. Weather permitting, I walk with him on the Glacis, then we dine at the 'Zum Bömischen Köchin,' which is the rendezvous of the Academy Students, and afterwards we go to one of the best coffee-houses. Then I make calls, get into my evening clothes, and perhaps go to some soirée. About eleven or twelve o'clock (never later) I come home, play, or read, and then go to bed.'

In his correspondence at this time we find frequent reference to Constantia, his love for whom

he does not seem yet to have got over. Moreover, at no time—no matter how depressed he
may have felt—did he allow his parents to think he
was anything but perfectly happy. To his friend he
says:—'If she (Constantia) mocks me, tell her the
same as my parents, namely, that I am very happy
and in want of nothing; but should she inquire kindly
for me, and show concern for me, whisper to her
that, away from her, I am ever lonely and unhappy.'

Amongst his most intimate friends at this time
was Dr. Malfatti, who had also been the friend of
Beethoven, whom he had attended on his death-
bed. Chopin was a frequent visitor at the doctor's
house, and in his letters we find great stress laid upon
the friendship existing between them. He frequently
dined at the doctor's, in reference to which he says,
'I am very brisk and in good health. Malfatti's soups
have strengthened me so much that I now feel better
than I ever did. Malfatti really loves me, and I am
not a little proud of it.' At Dr. Malfatti's house he
met the publisher Mechetti, to whom he handed for
publication the Polonaise of 'Cello and Piano, Op. 3.
Besides Haslinger and this Mechetti, Czerny was the

only publisher of importance in Vienna at the time, and it was with difficulty that Chopin was able to persuade them into publishing his works. ' *Waltzes*,' he says, 'are here called *works*, and it is almost waltzes alone that are published.' This is not difficult to credit, for we know the enormous hold which was obtained over the public by Strauss and Länner, with their compositions in this form. Every newspaper went into ecstasies over each new set of waltzes that was published, and the articles which appeared concerning these purveyors of dances and their *works* were certainly longer and more numerous than those which had been written concerning Mozart or Beethoven.

As we have seen, Chopin invariably kept his parents in the dark with regard to what he termed his ' misfortunes,' which, it must be owned, were often more the result of his own ' passive ' disposition than anything else. He was not a man to grasp opportunities, and humoured himself and his feelings to an extent which was frequently prejudicial ·to his interests. He had given no concert, simply because he had not been encouraged to do so by those to whom he was wont to look for advice in these matters. His father seems to have been much disappointed at this, and wrote remonstrating with him upon it. Chopin's only reply was, that it was his most fervent desire to fulfil his wishes, and to give a concert, but that hitherto he had found it impossible. He, however, played at a concert given by Madame Garzia-Vestris, having for fellow-artists Böhm the violinist, Merk, the brothers Lewy (horn-players), and the Misses Sabine and Clara Heinfetter. Whether it was that things were mismanaged, or not managed at all, we do not know; but Chopin, urged by the letter from his parents, did bestir himself, and gave a concert at this time, with the lamentable result that the expenses were greatly in excess of the receipts. Nor did he apply himself to his work of composition in any great degree, preferring to pass his time in social rather than artistic activity. Thus it is that these months spent in Vienna did little or nothing to increase his fame or name. On one or two occasions we find mention in his letters of his having finished some waltz or mazurka, but never does he speak seriously of his work. His attention and thoughts seem to have been directed more upon the question of ways and means. This may have been brought about partly by the failure of the concert; but, be that as it may, he was obliged to write to his parents for money to enable him to leave Vienna.

His departure from the Austrian capital took place in the latter part of July 1831, Chopin travelling in company with his friend Kumelski, to Paris *viâ* Salzburg and Munich. At the latter town he was obliged to wait monetary supplies from his parents. Assisted by several fellow-artists, he took advantage of this enforced interruption of his journey to give a concert, at which he played the E minor Concerto, and Fantasia on Polish airs. Of these compositions the press spoke highly, especially praising the Rondo movement of the Concerto. The journey to Paris was in due course continued, the next stop being made at Stuttgart. Here it was that he was informed of the capture by the Russians of his native city, which, as he says, 'caused him very great pain.' Having turned his back on Stuttgart, Chopin's career may be said,—so far as Germany is concerned,—to have ended.   Henceforth, Paris was to be his home, and there it is that we shall now leave him for a time, whilst in the meanwhile we direct our attention upon his work.   Those pieces which we shall proceed to notice are the Concerto in E minor, Op. 11, for piano and orchestra, the Fantasia, Op. 13, and the Concerto in F minor, Op. 21.

Seeing that Chopin adopted the strict Concerto form laid down by Mozart, it is surprising that the results of his work done in this form are so satisfactory.   The Mozart Concerto form is in itself unsurpassable as an example of pure classic form; but here, as in the case of piano technique, directly we enter upon the realm of romanticism, it is necessary it should be adapted to the requirements of the composer.   Beethoven himself led the way in this respect, as well as being the first to write his own cadenzas, instead of leaving them to the fancy of the pianist.   Mendelssohn also made innovations on the form, and since their time nearly every composer of note may be said to have added his 'quota' of modification.   Chopin, however, adhered to the strict form, taking Hummel as his immediate model. Insomuch as a great deal of the music of these works is 'virtuoso' music, he is in that more or less successful, but the great essential as regards the art of concerto writing is the artistic interweaving of the orchestra, with the principal solo instrument (in Chopin's case, the piano). It is in this respect we notice the great want in Chopin's Concertos. The piano music is frequently beautiful, but directly the orchestra makes its entry we are transferred to another atmosphere; granted that the master had no aptitude for the handling of masses of tone, and that his instrumentation was not worthy to stand by his pianoforte work, we have, in some cases, had his orchestral accompaniments re-scored by musicians who have made the art of instrumentation their special study, and who are naturally gifted in that direction. Even then their effect as regards the 'Tutti' is most unsatisfactory. Why? Because Chopin's musical ideas were not 'orchestral.' It is difficult for any one who has not written music to fully comprehend the great significance of that term as applied to any particular theme. Any two themes may be equally beautiful as abstract music. Yet one may be eminently orchestral, and the other purely piano music. We may even go further than this, and say that in the true composer for the orchestra every theme is conceived together with the instrument to which it should be allotted. This is the true basis of orchestration outside the bare technique, excellence in which is open to all; but the faculty of knowing to which instrument any particular theme belongs, is a gift, and Chopin was without it. We have already seen that the F minor Concerto was written before the one in E minor. But its publication did not take place until some time after; the respective dates of publication being, that of the E minor in 1833 and the F minor in 1836. It is to the former, however, that we propose first to direct our attention. In it we find two distinctly opposing forces at work, a leaning in the form towards classicism, yet over all an unmistakable presence of the romantic. The composer is continually pulling himself up, as much as to say, ' I am writing a Concerto, and must not let myself wander in this way.' Consequently, we cannot but be impressed with a sense of insincerity. It is strongly borne in upon us that we are in the presence of an *effort*; that the composer is striving to be what he felt he was not; to write what he did not feel,—in fact, that he is ‘manufacturing’ music. True, the old conventional concerto did much in itself to convey this impression, for had it not for its sole *raison d'être* the display of the technical capabilities of the performer? ‘Pianism’ was the essence of the Concerto. To-day we have changed all that. We treat the piano differently; its share is only part and parcel of the whole. The music allotted to the solo instrument is embodied with, and dependent for its existence upon, the remainder of the work; and although excellence of technique in the performer is a *sine qua non*, it is relegated to a decidedly secondary place. In short, a new variety has been developed from the antecedent type. And this is as it should be. For should not Art have Nature for its model? and does not Nature continually advance by this very development from antecedent types? Assuredly so. Did we rest content with a mere imitation of past forms we should

be true no more to Nature than we should be to
ourselves. The art forms of a past age are no longer
the art forms of our age, inasmuch as true art
should be the spontaneous outcome—in fact, the
direct expression—of the thought and culture of its
time. Our only dependence upon, and obligation to,
those past forms, is in that we retain such features
of them as are serviceable to our present requirements. In the Concerto this advancement has
happily taken place to a very large extent, and an
entirely new order of tone structure is the result.
But when we have regard to the state of the form
at the time when Chopin wrote, the only respect in
which we can reasonably look for him to excel is
in the direction of 'virtuoso' music. This, and this
only, it is that we get from him in his Concertos.
The idealisation, the individuality, in a word, the
advancement which is so prominent a feature of his
smaller work, is conspicuous only by its absence.
Of these smaller forms in which he wrote there was
no one which did not gain from his choice of it as
a medium of expression; indeed, in some cases, as,
for instance, in that of the *Etudes*, he so idealised

it as to remove it entirely from the category under which it formerly existed. The Ballade he created, albeit in it he can hardly be said to have bequeathed an art-form which has been used as a means of expression by other composers. It is as much a part of his individuality as the thought contained in it, and is merely a frame suitable for the enclosure of his ideas,—an adaptation to his æsthetic purpose, arising from emotional rather than any technical causes. Indeed, we may say that in the Concerto his subordination to, and inability to cope with, form was as conspicuous as was his superiority and independence of it in his smaller works. In the E minor Concerto we find in the first place the introductory *tutti*, in which the principal themes are announced to consist of 138 bars. This could have been contracted with advantage. It opens with an introductory phrase ($\frac{3}{4}$ time) of four bars, in which the melody is given to the first violins, being strengthened by the entry of the flutes at the last beat of the second bar. The same phrase repeated in the key of the sub-dominant is followed by several fragmentary phrases, leading us to the first subject in E minor. This melody is sustained wholly by the first violins,. accompanied by the remainder of the strings. Twenty bars later we have a phrase imitatory of that with which the pianoforte makes its first entry. This is given to bassoons, trombones, 'celli, and basses, accompanied only by strings. On the announcement, sixteen bars later, of the second subject in E major, the strings again sustain both melody and accompaniment, until we have proceeded some ten bars, when the horns enter. At the subsidiary section we get relief by the allotment of the melody to the flutes and bassoons, which eight bars later give place to the violins and flutes, with string and wood-wind accompaniments. The pianoforte enters to an accompaniment of strings *pizzicato*, and after some bars of passage-work we get to work on the first subject in E minor. After twenty-four bars comes one of the most delicate and delightful bits of writing in the work. This is at the *tranquillo* semi-quaver passages. After more passage-work, the second subject in E major is reached, and eight bars later there occurs an effective entry of the E horn, sustaining portions of the harmony, in the accompaniment. The melody is now smooth and straight-forward, but not particularly Chopinesque. At the *appassionato*, the strings, sustaining dotted minims, form an effective contrast to the piano part, the melody of which proceeds in octaves. At the *agitato*, strings in the accompaniment give way to clarinets, bassoons, and horns. Following the *tutti*, we have what is evidently intended for a ' working-out ' section in C major, but here clarity cannot be said to reign ; indeed, there is much that savours of confusion. Shortly before the return to the initial theme in E minor, the *tutti* enters with its opening phrase. The next appearance of the second subject is in the key of G major, and is followed by an amount of passage-work, by means of which we are led to the close of the movement in the tonic E minor.

But it may be asked, What is the æsthetic effect of all this ? To this we can only reply in one word—unsatisfactory. Besides the reasons we have already assigned for this, we may add another : the want of key-contrast. The monotony felt by the adherence for so long to the same tonality, and the absolute floundering about by the composer in the working-out section, is not in any way relieved by the treatment of the solo instrument. The orchestra never gets seriously to work, whilst there is a lack of freshness in the material, and of piquancy in its treatment. That spontaneity for which we are so accustomed to look is conspicuous only by its absence. Nor do things improve to any appreciable extent in the *larghetto* and *rondo*, beyond the fact that a good effect is gained by their contrast.

When we remember the circumstances under which he wrote, and the ' Ideal ' who inspired it, we wonder that there is so little of real inspiration in the former movement; for it cannot be compared to the corresponding portion in the companion concerto in F minor. It exhales a sickly sweetness which causes us to long for a purer atmosphere. This we get to a certain degree in *rondo*; but here, again, we are frequently in contemplation of the commonplace, whilst the intervening orchestral snatches simply worry by their triviality. Nevertheless we cannot lose sight, in this movement, of some very delicate detail in the pianoforte part, which has its due effect.

We might also draw attention to the modulation from E major to E flat major, which is particularly exhilarating and fresh. But we are lingering somewhat unduly, perhaps, on this work, and must pass on to the consideration of the Fantaisie and the F minor Concerto.

The former of these is chiefly interesting as containing variations of some very characteristic Polish melodies. The introduction of them is sometimes more or less abrupt, and in treatment they are not subjected to the same amount of refinement of workmanship as we find, for instance, in one of his latest works, the Berceuse, where the form of variation is much the same. On the other hand, what orchestration there is here, better fulfils its object than in other of his works, and although it cannot be said to possess any great artistic value, the work is decidedly interesting to the pianoforte player.

In the F minor Concerto, the first thing that strikes us is the greater directness of purpose, which shows itself in the introduction. It is altogether less wandering and more compact, and is not in any way marred by its orchestral treatment. Indeed, the instrumentation is here concise and frequently tasteful. The pianoforte passage-work, although demanding much in the way of technique from the performer, is much more effective, and repays to a much greater extent the labour expended upon it than that in the E minor work. The second subject is most beautiful, both in its natural and ornate states; and the whole of the first movement more satisfying in every way. Exquisite, also, in its way, is the *larghetto,* with its recitative passages and delicate *fioriture.* Here we cannot refrain from singling out the following theme,

which is of surpassing beauty, but which is only one of the many beauties to be found in this movement. It is far and away the most spiritual piece of work Chopin has given us in any of his compositions for piano and orchestra. The accompaniment of this phrase is for strings only *sostenuto*, the recitative following being accompanied by the strings *tremolo*, with the exception of the basses, which are playing *pizzicato*. Of the finale it is impossible to speak in terms of unqualified praise, but whatever is lacking is more than compensated for by the lovely movement which we have just noticed. Finally, while we can only feel regret at the non-success of our artist in handling these more important forms of composition, yet to him in his endeavour to do so we must be thankful, if only because of his failure therein he was induced to abandon them, and to confine himself the more particularly to those smaller forms in which he has given us so much of the beautiful.

CHAPTER VI

PARIS was in 1831, as it is to-day, one of the greatest art centres in the world. From the beginning of the century the influence of the Revolution on art had been making itself felt. The works of Shakespeare, Schiller, and Goethe opened out an entirely new field to the authors of the drama in France. In the art of poetry, side by side with Victor Hugo, Lamartine, Alfred de Musset, and André Chénier, there was still room for such as Alfred de Vigny and Pierre de Béranger; while in the sister art of painting were Delacroix, Delaroche, Ary Scheffer, and Géricault. With all these working for the cause of romanticism, the sister art of music could not but be influenced very considerably thereby, and one of the most direct and emphatic results of it was the creation by Hector Berlioz of the Symphonie Fantastique. Fortunately for the Romantic school it had no half-hearted partisan in Hector Berlioz. He not only possessed all the qualities necessary to enable him to combat and overcome the many obstacles and trials which stand in the way of the innovator, but he possessed genius sufficient to force a considerable part of his public to admit that his music was capable without stage accessories, or assistance from words, of expressing not only definite emotions, but of bringing before them a picture very little less vivid than that to which they were accustomed in the theatre. From this time forward we can trace the development of the symphonic art in France. Hitherto, apart from a few works from such men as Cherubini, Méhul, and Le Sueur, the symphony had been almost totally neglected in that country. From the symphony in turn we can trace the birth and development of the French lyric drama, of which such brilliant examples have been given to the world by Georges Bizet, M. Charles Gounod, M. Massenet, M. Lalo, and M. Reyer,—musicians who have raised France to the head of all contemporary dramatic music.

But to return to our period. The operatic composers then writing, such as Meyerbeer, Auber, Herold and Boieldieu, were fortunate enough to have as the exponents of their work such artists as Malibran, Pasta, Rubini, and Lablache. To Paris came artists from all parts of the world. There, and there only, was it possible for a reputation to be made, and the hall-mark of success secured. Therefore was Chopin fortunate in being associated with artists of pretensions and capacities not inferior to his own.

He had come to Paris with letters of introduction to various publishers, and also to the composer Frederic Paër, who had written several successful works, the most prominent of which was *Le Maître de Chapelle*, produced at the Opéra Comique in 1821 with great success. By this means Chopin made the acquaintance of Cherubini, Rossini, and Kalkbrenner, and later we find him the central figure of a small *coterie* of artists gathered together at this time in the French capital. Amongst them we may mention Mendelssohn, Hiller, Liszt, and Franchomme the violoncellist.

Hitherto, as we have seen, Chopin had outside of Paris achieved considerable success as a pianist, but Parisians were wont to look upon foreign *critiques* of matters musical as of little worth, and as he felt himself capable of improvement in this branch of his profession he decided to place himself in the hands of Kalkbrenner, who at that time was looked upon as the foremost master in the world.

In a letter to his friend Woyciechowski, he relates very minutely his visit to the famous pianist. He had recently heard him play, and waxes most enthusiastic over 'his enchanting touch, his repose and smoothness in playing.' On Chopin visiting him, Kalkbrenner naturally wished him to play. 'What was I to do?' says Chopin. 'As I had heard Herz, I plucked up courage and played my E minor Concerto.' Kalkbrenner was astonished, and straightway asked the young musician if he was a pupil of Field, remarking, at the same time, that he had the style of Cramer, but the touch of Field. Says Chopin:—'He proposed to teach me for three years, and to make a great artist of me, but I do not wish to be an imitation of him, and three years is too long a time for me. . . . After having watched me attentively, he came to the conclusion that I

H

had no method; that although I was at present in a very fair way, I might easily go astray, and that when *he* ceased to play, there would no longer be a representative of the grand old pianoforte school left. I cannot create a new school, however much I may wish to do so, because I am not yet master of the old one, but I know that my tone-poems have some individuality in them, and that my object is always to advance.' Considerably perplexed by this interview with Kalkbrenner, Chopin sought advice from his old friend and master, Joseph Elsner, who was much astonished at the opinion pronounced by Kalkbrenner, and replied asking him why he should place himself under the pianist who would only destroy his originality, and who was, he considered, unable to teach Chopin anything in pianoforte playing. Besides, said Elsner, after all, pianoforte playing is not by any means the end of the art, and the achievements of Mozart and Beethoven in this direction have long been overshadowed by their greater accomplishments as composers. ' In a word,' he goes on, ' that quality in an artist (who continually learns from what is around him), which excites the wonder of his contemporaries, can only arrive at perfection by and through himself. The cause of his fame, whether in the present or the future, is none other than his own gifted individuality manifested in his works.' In his reply to this letter, Chopin says:—'Although, as Kalkbrenner himself has admitted, three years' study is far too much, I would willingly make up my mind to even that length of time, were I sure that in the end I should attain my object. But one thing is quite clear to me, and that is, that I shall never be a mere *réplique* of Kalkbrenner.' He then goes on to prove to his master how such men as Spohr and Ries were obliged to make their fame as masters of their respective instruments the stepping-stone to their fame as composers.

Elsner had put forth the assumption that Kalkbrenner's desire to keep Chopin in the background for three years was actuated by jealousy, but it does not seem to us that such was the case, for the reason that the pianist's reputation was not one to be easily superseded. Moreover, it was no more than natural that a master of the pianoforte such as he was, as regards technique, should be considerably taken aback by innovations in fingering, etc., made use of by Chopin, all which he would naturally regard as solecisms. Again, we know that it was the invariable rule of Kalkbrenner to accept no pupil for a less term than three years. Whether or not Chopin's friends were correct in saying that he played better than Kalkbrenner we are not prepared to say, but that Elsner was wrong in saying that he (Chopin) could learn nothing from him we do say, for the fusion of the ideas of two men, the antithesis in art of each other —such as these two were—cannot but be beneficial in its results to both. Eventually Chopin discontinued his visits, and took no more lessons from Kalkbrenner; nevertheless, he remained on friendly terms with the pianist, as is shown by the dedication to him of the E minor Concerto.

In a letter, dated the 6th December 1831, we find Chopin announcing to his friend Titus his intention of giving a concert in Paris on the 25th of the same month. In the arrangements of this he was assisted by Kalkbrenner, Paër, and Norblin the violoncellist. These preliminaries were a source of great annoyance and difficulty to him, and for the carrying out of them such assistance was indispensable. The chief trouble seems to have been in finding a suitable vocalist. All the best were in the hands of the Operatic Directors, who refused to allow artists under engagement to them to assist, fearing that if they did so on this occasion they would be besieged on all quarters by similar requests. For this and other reasons the concert had to be postponed until the 15th January following, and even then it was not destined to take place, for Kalkbrenner's being suddenly taken ill necessitated a further postponement to the 26th February. In the end he was assisted by Baillot the violinist (the rival of Paganini), Brod, a celebrated oboe player, while the vocalists were Mlles. Isambert, Toméoni, and M. Boulanger.

In a letter of Chopin's, about this date, he expresses his intention of playing at the concert the F minor Concerto and the Variations in B flat, and with Kalkbrenner, the latter's 'Marche suivie d'une Polonaise,' for two pianos, with accompaniment for four others. 'On the other ones,' he says, 'which are as loud as any orchestra, Hiller, Osborne, Stamati, and Sowinski will play.' Whatever success may have attended this concert artistically, it was financially a disastrous failure. Since his arrival in Paris Chopin had made his home and acquaintances mostly amongst the Polish refugees at that time in the city, and, as a natural consequence, they formed the largest section of his audience; such musicians and fellow-artists as were present did not, of course, contribute towards the expenses. Nevertheless, it was the means of revealing to the musicians present (amongst whom was Felix Mendelssohn) the great originality of Chopin. The critic, François Fétis, speaking of Chopin's music in a notice of this concert, said that he found in it 'an abundance of original idea of a type to be found nowhere else'; and also 'the indication of a renewal of forms which might in time exercise no small influence over his special branch of art'; while he characterises his playing as 'elegant, easy, and graceful, and possessing great brilliance and neatness.' Therefore, although of no assistance to him financially, this concert did much to give him a reputation amongst those whose opinion was valuable, and who were, moreover, in a position to distribute it.

From his letters at this time it can be seen that he was in no very cheerful frame of mind; and a great longing to return to his own country would at times come over him. Outwardly he was bright enough, only unburdening himself of his real feelings to his friend Titus. Nevertheless even to him he would occasionally write cheerfully enough. For instance, in the postscript of one of these letters we have him joking over a little *affaire d'amour* with a pretty neighbour, Francilla Pixis by name, for whom he seems to have conceived a very violent passing fancy; and, no doubt, the cheery side of his nature would have asserted itself strongly enough had his financial position been more satisfactory. He was determined not to be any burden to his parents, who, although in comfortable circumstances, were by no means wealthy. He found it impossible to get on in Paris at that time as quickly as he would have wished, in fact as was absolutely necessary he should do, and as a natural consequence began to look about him in order to see the best method of

ameliorating his position. At length he resolved
to join a party of his countrymen and to emigrate
to America; and, ludicrous as it would seem, he
would most assuredly have carried out this mad
project, notwithstanding the earnest solicitation of
his parents to the contrary. They were naturally
anxious to prevent such a thing, knowing full well
how little fitted for such a life he was. They
urged him to return to Warsaw, and he had all
but decided to fall in with their wishes, when
he was prevented from doing so by one of those
curious chances which often go so far to rule
the lives of men. Shortly before his intended departure he happened to meet his friend Prince
Radziwill, to whom he confided his intention of
leaving Paris. The prince had always been fond of
Chopin, and greeted him warmly on this occasion.
On hearing of his latest resolve he did not try to
dissuade him from it directly; but knowing full
well the state of things which had been instrumental in bringing it about, he wisely and kindly
thought of a practical means by which to prevent
it, not by mere persuasion, but by showing the

young musician that it was to his interest to remain. Accordingly he extracted from Chopin a promise to accompany him to a soirée which was to be given at the house of his friends, the Rothschilds, on the following evening. To this he agreed. The result was that he played and delighted the whole company, and left the richer by several promises of pupils, and the high opinion of those who could be of substantial benefit to him. Mr. Frederick Niecks hazards a doubt as to the truth of this story. He says that neither Liszt, Hiller, nor Franchomme knew anything of it. Perhaps not; in fact, we do not think it probable that Chopin would be likely to make a point of mentioning it, as one of his greatest characteristics was pride, and perhaps of all his faults, the most glaring was what would seem to be ingratitude, but what was very frequently nothing but thoughtlessness. Moreover, it was just the sort of thing to be expected from Prince Radziwill, and it further accounts in a very satisfactory manner for his remaining in Paris. However, be that as it may, from this time forward dates Chopin's success in society and as a teacher.

We purpose, before closing this chapter, to take for consideration a group of compositions in which Chopin excelled, and showed the sentimental side of his genius to a greater extent perhaps than in any other, namely—the Nocturnes. There are eighteen tone-poems which we get under this head. Especially notable here are the unique *fiorituri*, an embellishment which Chopin handled marvellously when we consider how quickly it would nauseate in the hands of many composers. In fact, with him the difference lay in that these, in his mind, were frequently not so much embellishments as part of the whole conception. We find in the catalogue of his works the following: Op. 9, three Nocturnes; Op. 15, three Nocturnes; Op. 27, two Nocturnes; Op. 32, two Nocturnes; Op. 37, two Nocturnes; Op. 48, two Nocturnes; Op. 55, two Nocturnes; and likewise two more under Op. 62. Besides which there is a posthumous publication by Julius Fontana, numbered Op. 72, which contains, together with a Funeral March and three Ecossaises, a Nocturne in E minor. Of the Op. 9, Heinrich Rellstab,—editor of the Berlin musical journal *Iris*, and one of the most hostile of critics towards Chopin,—wrote that it closely resembled the Nocturnes of John Field as regards melody and manner of accompaniment. But either the critic was not happy in the expression of his meaning, or he showed a terrible lack of insight. If we grant that Chopin took the 'genus' from Field this is as far as we can possibly go; for any two composers between whom there is—as regards emotional expression—a wider gulf could not be found. In the Nocturne of Field we have pretty melody, but very shallow, and frequently the accompaniments are commonplace and wearisome in the extreme. When Chopin took the 'Nocturne' in hand he invested it with an elegance and depth of meaning which had never been given to it before. The No. 1 in B flat minor is especially remarkable for this, and is by turns voluptuous and dramatic; it was certainly not in the cold nature of Field to pen such bars as the sixteenth and seventeenth of this work. A couple of bars later there occurs a phrase, which we look upon as one of the most purely 'Chopinesque' that the master ever wrote.

We refer to :—

As an example of pure, unaffected, and beautiful music he has never surpassed this phrase. Notice in the next bar how the sadness is intensified by the enharmonic change. Again, what could be more *triste* than the phrase in D flat, which occurs some thirty-four bars later, marked *legatissimo*? After a return to the initial theme he brings the work to a close with the chord of the tonic major. The second of the same opus is so well-known as to render any comment needless. We only point out another instance of the composer's partiality to a succession of chords of the seventh (*vide* bar 12). It is æsthetically and psychologically inferior to its companions, and savours somewhat of affectation. The same might also be said, though perhaps in a lesser degree, of the third number. Of the 1st of Op. 15 in F major, the most remarkable portion is the *con fuoco* movement, which gains much by the contrast it forms with the *andante cantabile*. But in the following number in F sharp major, we have again one of the most important of the group. The ear is struck with the placid beauty of the opening phrase, and the *fiorituri* here are thrown about most lavishly. The scene is changed when we reach the *doppio movimento*, and dramatic energy holds sway for a time, after which the placidity of the first portion prevails until the close. The Nocturne in C sharp minor, the first of Op. 27, is perhaps the most dramatic of all. It opens with a yearning *larghetto sotto voce*, with a sextuplet quaver accompaniment, mostly on a double pedal, and proceeds calmly until the ninth bar is reached, when, instead of preceding the leading note and rising to the tonic as it did in the fifth bar, there is silence for a whole bar, the accompaniment only being heard, while the thread dropped is taken up in the following bar. Notice also in the thirteenth bar from the commencement the communicating effect of the D natural, which is especially accented.

The very first bar of the *più mosso* movement is ominous. And here we will call the reader's attention to the wonderful effect obtained in these twenty bars, with the simplest of means. Let us for the moment look somewhat closely into them. The whole section we find to consist of the first four bars repeated alternately in the tonic and dominant keys, with the exception of the last four bars, which for our purpose we may call supplementary. If we look into the material of which this phrase of four bars is constructed, we shall find it to consist of merely the first and second inversions of the dominant seventh chord, resolved in each case on the tonic. By this means, it will be noticed, the bass progresses steadily upwards, and, by so doing, greatly heightens the effect. (When it reaches the B sharp octave above which it started it proceeds in octaves.) The last four bars of the section take us into the key of A flat major. Such are the means employed by Chopin to produce a most vivid tone picture. Higher art than this one could not have, if simplicity of means be a factor of high art. But we have dwelt somewhat unduly upon this work, and must hurry on. The second of this opus in D flat is one of the most frequently heard in our concert rooms. It abounds in much that is characteristic of his pianoforte music, such as the lavish use of sixths in the right hand and indulgence in *fioriture,* and if it has not the same depth of meaning as that which we have just discussed, it is one of the most delicate and sweet of the Nocturnes, though it is more notable for the excessive elaboration of the detail than for the musical material of which it is composed.

We now come to the first of the Op. 32. It is in the key of B major. After the minute elaboration of the last one, the simplicity here strikes us most forcibly.

Notice in this Nocturne the sudden arrest of the

melody in a manner somewhat similar to that in the
C sharp minor one.　It occurs at the sixth bar :—

and seems as if the composer wished to make us
reflect for a moment, after which he leads us on to
the close of the phrase by a cadence as delicious
as it is simple.　Nothing now disturbs the even
flow of the melody until we are nearing the end,
when we meet with an interrupted cadence, followed by a recitative of some length, with which
the work closes.　The next in A flat major opens
in a particularly simple and straightforward manner,
and we find nothing to call for notice until we come
to the second section in the relative minor, where
we have the time changed to $\frac{12}{8}$, and a succession
of quaver chords which grow more passionate and
wailing when the octaves are reached at the ninth
bar.　The same section is then repeated in the key

of F sharp minor, at the close of which we reach the initial theme in A flat, which forms the last portion of the work. In Op. 37 we get two Nocturnes of exceptional beauty—the first in G minor, and the second in G major. Notice the hymn-like plain chord progression of the middle section of No. 1, and the exceptional beauty of the melody in the first part, whilst the opening bars of the G major Nocturne perhaps justify the title more than any we have yet met. The rocking, sensuous motion of the quaver figure in the bass, the succession of thirds and sixths in the right hand, and the numerous transitions through remote keys are the chief features of the work. The second section in the key of the sub-dominant reappears later on in that of the sub-mediant. It is a very lovely theme this, and if we look into it we find it is simplicity itself. I think a careful study of such works of Chopin's as these Nocturnes will go far to do away with a very prevalent notion that his musical thoughts were complicated; on the contrary, we find here, as with many others of the masters of music, that the most beautiful are frequently the most simple.

I

Of the two Nocturnes in C minor and C sharp minor which go to make up the Op. 48, it is not possible to speak enthusiastically, as when they are not sickly they are laboured, especially so in the last movement *doppio movimento* of the first named, whilst the relief offered by the *più lento* of the one in C sharp minor is not sufficient, and the section is in itself very fragmentary. We would point out the enharmonic modulation at bar eighteen and nineteen of this section as perhaps one of the most happy thoughts in it. Things do not change much for the better until we reach No. 1 of Op. 62. The opening two bars are sufficiently original, and the melody which follows, although hardly one of the best, is inexpressibly sweet. A change is welcome at the *sostenuto* in A flat. This section ends on the E flat chord, the E flat being changed enharmonically to the third of the chord of B major, and the initial phrase presented to us in this key surrounded with all kinds of embellishment. Considerable harmonic cunning is evinced in this Nocturne, but the whole lacks that spontaneity which so distinguishes some of the earlier ones.

CHAPTER VII

ONCE having made up his mind to remain in Paris,
Chopin soon became a prominent figure in society.
Since the evening when he had played at the
Rothschild soirée, he had been fortunate enough to
secure several pupils, and as they increased so was
his position financially benefited. The five years commencing from this time were perhaps the happiest
and most brilliant of his life. He enjoyed in a great
measure the delights of success and the satisfaction
of having in some degree realised his ambitions. He
was now frequently to be heard playing in public,
and amongst the concerts at which he assisted at
this time we may name one given by Hiller in
December 1832, and also one in the following year
given by the brothers Herz, besides numerous private
functions at which he assisted. Let us for a moment
consider Liszt's picture of the master at this period.

He says : 'The *ensemble* of his person was harmonious, and called for no special commentary. His blue [1] eye was more spiritual than dreamy; his bland smile never writhed into bitterness. The transparent delicacy of his complexion pleased the eye; his fair hair was soft and silky, his nose slightly aquiline, his bearing so distinguished, and his manner stamped with so much of high breeding, that involuntarily he was always treated *en prince*. He was generally gay, his caustic spirit caught the ridiculous rapidly, and far below the surface at which it usually strikes the eye. His gaiety was so much the more piquant, because he always restrained it within the bounds of good taste, holding at a distance all that might tend to wound the most fastidious delicacy.' Also would we draw attention to what his friend Orlowski wrote of him. 'Chopin is full of health and vigour; all the Frenchwomen dote upon him, and all the men are jealous of him. In a word, he is the fashion, and we shall, no doubt, shortly have gloves *à la* Chopin.'

These comments from two men, who both were

[1] Here Liszt was wrong, as Chopin had brown eyes.

intimates of Chopin, do not tend to convey that extreme femininity with which even this, perhaps the most energetic part of his life, has been coloured by some of his biographers. There is no doubt that his nature was more akin to the feminine than the masculine; nevertheless, this characteristic has, in most cases, been considerably overdrawn and exaggerated. He, it must be remembered, suffered much, in common with his race, from political oppression; and, also, that not only had he within him the seeds of an hereditary disease, but hitherto his financial position had not been such as to engender any unusual brightness of spirit. These things, acting together upon his extremely reserved nature, no doubt rendered him at times liable to be greatly misunderstood by any casual observer. But from what we know from his intimate friends, it is far from right to colour the master's life with the sombre and unrelieved tints with which it has so often been painted. Further proof we have from the companion of his youth, Johannes Matuszynski, who, having served as a surgeon-major in the Polish army and taken his doctor's degree, had just been appointed professor in the School of Medicine at Paris. Arrived there, he says, 'The first thing I did was to find out Chopin, and I cannot describe what great pleasure it gave us both to meet again after our separation of five years. He has grown so strong and tall that I scarcely knew him. Chopin is now the first of pianists in Paris; he gives a great many lessons, at twenty francs each, and is altogether in great request. We live together here at the Rue Chausée d'Antin, No. 5.'

Here we have direct testimony of the improvement in his physique, not only from an old friend, but from a physician. Although so much in request, Chopin was not in any way blinded by the eulogies lavished upon him by all and sundry. He well knew that many of his aristocratic acquaintances were entirely ignorant of the veriest rudiments of his art, and praised him solely because he happened to be the fashion. Writing to a friend, he says, 'I move in the highest society. I take my place amidst ambassadors, princes, ministers; and I have not the least notion how I got there, for it was no doing of mine. Nevertheless, I find all this at present absolutely necessary, for one is credited with so much more talent when one has received the applause of the English or Austrian Ambassador, and there is so much more *finesse* about one's playing if one happens to secure the patronage of the Princess Vaudemont.'   Severe; but surely true, and it is well he had sufficient strength of mind to recognise it, and nothing shows us how thorough an artist Chopin was more than what he says later on in the same letter: 'Really, if I happened to be a little more silly than I am, I might almost be led to imagine myself a finished artist.   As it is, I only feel how much I have still to learn, and recognise it the more when, having daily intercourse, as I have, with all the first artists here, I recognise how much even they lack.'

His great rival, and the one musician against whom he was being continually pitted, was John Field.   Yet Chopin not only possessed all the gifts of Field, but supplied those in which the latter was found wanting.   As Moscheles said of Field:— His playing lacked spirit and accent, light and shade, and depth of feeling.   All these Chopin supplied in an extraordinary degree, and in them he excelled. In composition, the older master only furnished us with a hint of what we were to receive from Chopin, and this is so very slight that we cannot in any way look upon him as the forerunner of Chopin's style. He was as distinct from it as any other musician. The Nocturnes he wrote were not even shadows of Chopin's Nocturnes, beside which they might easily be called vulgar, as compared with those of the Polish master. John Field, on his part, no doubt saw in Chopin only a formidable rival, very likely to ruin the lustre of his own glory; at all events, he tried to dismiss Chopin lightly, by saying that he possessed only *un talent de chambre de malade.* Such a statement was not for one moment worth serious consideration; nevertheless, Chopin's compositions at this time met with serious opposition on the part of several of the musical critics. His greatest enemy in this respect was Rellstab, critic of the *Iris,* who, for instance, in writing a notice of one of the Mazurkas, said of Chopin:—'He is indefatigable, I might almost say inexhaustible, in his search for ear-splitting discords, forced transitions,

harsh modulations, horrible distortions of melody
and rhythm.   Everything is done to produce the
effect of peculiar originality, by such means as out-
of-the-way keys, and chords in unnatural positions.'
Finally he says:—' Had M. Chopin shown this composition to a master, the latter would, there is no
doubt, have torn it up and thrown it at his feet,
which we hereby do symbolically for him.'

The only comparison this unenlightened creature
draws between Chopin and Field we quote for what
it is worth :—' Where Field smiles, Chopin makes a
grimace ; where Field sighs, Chopin groans ; where
Field shrugs his shoulders, Chopin twists his whole
body. . . . In short, if one holds Field's charming
romances before a distorting concave mirror, so that
every delicate expression becomes coarse, one gets
Chopin's music. . . . We beg of M. Chopin to return
to nature.'   Anent this, Mr. Niecks quotes a letter
which was supposed to have been written by Chopin
—when irate at this abuse—to the critic himself.
Mr. Niecks, however, states that he does not vouch
for its authenticity; nevertheless, parts of it will
no doubt interest the reader.   The commencement

is noteworthy. It says:—' You are really a very bad man, and not worthy that God's earth either knows or bears you. The King of Music should have imprisoned you in a fortress; in that case he would have removed from the world a rebel, a disturber of the peace, and an infamous enemy of humanity who probably will yet be choked in his own blood.' And even more vehement is the concluding phrase. ' Another bad, bad trick, and you are done for! Do you understand me, you little man, you loveless and partial dog of a critic, you musical snarler, you Berlin wit-cracker ?'

It cannot be said that Rellstab was alone in giving vent to adverse criticism of Chopin's works, for Moscheles, himself a thorough musician, disliked what he called the ' artificial and forced modulations ' which he met with in them; and Mendelssohn did not give them unqualified praise, as he held that Chopin aimed too often at ' sensationalism,' and disregarded true musical feeling. But seeing that there could hardly have been two musicians more antithetical of each other than were Chopin and Mendelssohn, what one would take

to be ' true' in regard to music, the other in many
cases would not. Therefore we may assume that
Mendelssohn was merely not in sympathy with
Chopin's genius, rather than that he took any determined stand against it.

In the spring of this year, 1834, Chopin, in company with Hiller, paid a short visit to Aix-la-
Chapelle on the occasion of the Lower Rhenish
Musical Festival, which was held there at Whitsun-
tide. Amongst others there they met Mendelssohn,
the three musicians witnessing the Festival together,
and seeing much of each other. Mendelssohn
was at this time occupying the post of Musical
Director at Düsseldorf, whither, after the Festival,
Chopin and Hiller accompanied him, and spent a
day in the town pleasantly enough. They were
asked to spend the evening—as they were to start
for Coblenz on the morrow—at the house of F. W.
Schadow, the Director of the Academy of Art at
Düsseldorf. Writing of this, Hiller says:—'For the
evening we were invited to Schadow's, who was
always hospitable, and where we found some of the
most eminent of rising young artists. The conversa-

tion soon became lively, and all would have been well had not poor Chopin sat so silent and unnoticed. However, both Mendelssohn and I knew that he would have his revenge, and were secretly rejoicing thereat. At last the piano was opened. I began, Mendelssohn followed, and then Chopin was asked to play, rather doubtful looks being cast at him and us. But he had scarcely played a few bars, when every one present, especially Schadow, assumed a very different attitude towards him. They had never heard anything like it, and all were in the greatest delight, and begged for more and more. Count Almaviva had dropped his disguise, and all were speechless.'

After Chopin's return to Paris we find him assisting at the last of a series of concerts given in the Conservatoire by Hector Berlioz, where he played the middle movement of the Concerto in F minor. Later in the same year we have him assisting Dr. Stoepel, an author of several works of music and on musical subjects, at a matinée; and in March 1835 Chopin played at a concert given by Pleyel, his fellow-artists being Herz, Osborne, Hiller, and Reicha.

In the early part of this same year, about April, he gave a concert for the benefit of the Polish refugees in Paris, at which Habeneck conducted, and Chopin played the E minor Concerto, and Hiller's duet for two pianos with Liszt, but the result was not wholly successful so far as either Chopin or the Concerto was concerned. Both the audience and the place were large, neither condition favourable to Chopin. He never played well under such circumstances; the public *en masse* intimidated him, and took from him that subtle power which so charmed when he played to an intimate circle of acquaintances. He himself said to Liszt:—'I am not at all fit for giving concerts; the crowd intimidates me; its breath suffocates me; I feel paralysed by its strange look, and the sea of unknown faces makes me dumb.'

At this time, foremost amongst Chopin's friends in Paris, was the Italian composer, Vincent Bellini, for whom he had a great friendship, and with whose music he was much in sympathy. Indeed, Bellini's influence upon Chopin can be clearly traced in some of his music, and we shall have occasion to refer to it in speaking of his songs.

Of the Italian master's work, *I Puritani*, which was
in this year produced at the Opera, and *Norma*, were
especial favourites with Chopin. In spite of his
many engagements, social and otherwise, as well as
his pupils, who took a great portion of his time,
Chopin was most assiduous in his devotion to composition. Amongst the works finished during his
first year in Paris were the Nocturnes, the Etudes,
Op. 10 and 25; the Bolero, Op. 19; the Scherzo,
Op. 20; Ballade, Op. 23; besides some Mazurkas
and Impromptus. It will suffice if, as well as taking
one group for notice here, we consider such isolated
pieces as the Bolero, and Polonaise, Op. 22. The
Bolero, Op. 19, is one of the least interesting of his
compositions. It has little or nothing beyond its
outward form to substantiate its title, and even had
it been written after instead of before the composer's
sojourn in the South, it would probably have still
lacked local colour. The *allegro vivace* has the form
and figure of the Bolero, but that is all; the spirit of
the dance is not there. Consequently the piece is
laboured and unsatisfactory.

We now turn to the Grande Polonaise, Op. 22, for

piano and orchestra. The Polonaise proper is preceded by an *Andante Spianato*, and is not worthy to stand beside the Polonaise for pianoforte alone. Neither can the *Andante* be said to be wholly satisfactory, and whether it was really composed with the intention of its preceding the *Bravura* movement seems doubtful. At all events the one has nothing whatever to connect it with the other, musically speaking. The melody of the first movement strikes us as closely resembling that of the Prelude No. 15. The key of the *Andante* is G major, while the polonaise itself is in E flat, and it is in the connecting modulatory portion that we have one of the noisiest and least artistic pieces of work to be found in any of Chopin's compositions. The *Andante* having ended with the tonic chord, the orchestra enters in order to effect the modulation to the new key. The note G in the following marked rhythm of the Polonaise is given to the E flat horn

in octaves, and is followed by a succession of chromatic chords on a pedal point for two bars, which are chiefly sustained by the wood, wind, and strings. After this a desperate struggle takes place, and lands us quite breathless on the dominant seventh of the E flat key. This chord we then have in its various inversions, and we are taken to be all ready for the entry of the pianoforte with the initial figure of the Polonaise. It is difficult, indeed, to comprehend how a musician, usually so careful and even original in such matters, could have allowed such a passage to escape him. But, alas! even now that we have emerged from this chaos, it is only to be confronted with a phrase which might have been constructed for some showy and tricky fiddler to beguile his unoffending and long-suffering audience with. But to do the composer justice, we are bound to say that he put forward this composition simply for what it was worth as a showy *salon* piece.

It is with relief that we turn to the contemplation of such vastly different works as are contained in the next group which we have selected, the four works which we get under the title of *Scherzo* affording us little that is not beautiful and original.

Applied to individual instrumental pieces, the Scherzo is synonymous of the *capriccio*, which must not be confounded with the *caprice*; the term originally applied to a movement in which a particular musical subject is handled in every conceivable manner by its composer. The Scherzo or Capriccio was a form greatly affected by Mendelssohn, whose light and airy muse it suited admirably. It gradually, in the hands of Beethoven, took the place in the Sonata form of the Minuet. But like other forms in which Chopin chose to express his musical thoughts, it underwent in his hands idealisation,—assumed an aspect of individual importance. From him we get four important works under this title. The Op. 20 in B minor, dedicated to M. Albrecht; the Op. 31 in B flat minor, to Mlle. de Fürstenstein; the Op. 39 in C sharp minor, to his friend and pupil Adolph Gutmann; and the fourth Op. 54 in E minor, to Mlle. de Caraman. Of the first in B minor we are struck by the opening chords. Surely, we say, this is not the commencement of a Scherzo! Certainly not to such a movement as Mendelssohn has accustomed us to under the name. Even the following measures express 'fury' rather than that of capriciousness. After a while the vigour of the rushing quaver figure becomes gradually less, until we come to the repeat. The middle movement in the tonic major has a melody in the inner part, surmounted by an inverted dominant pedal. The effect gained does not, to my mind, compensate for the excessive use of it. It is inexpressibly sweet for a few bars, but after that one experiences a sickly sensation. Neither is the melody characterised by the amount of finesse and refinement of handling we usually find and are accustomed to look for, the close on the dominant and return to the tonic in bars seven and eight of the *molto più lento* movement verging on the commonplace. After this we get nothing very new, and the work closes with a rush of chromatics in unison. It is not by any means one of his best efforts, seeming to be wanting in parts in melody and clearness, though it is undoubtedly brilliant.

No. 2 in B flat minor is a work far more concise and highly finished than that which we

have just discussed. It seems to open with two
distinct questions and answers, after the repetition of which, and a few bars of descending
and ascending quaver figures alternately, *ff.* and
pp., we come to the principal theme, which commences on the harmony of the dominant seventh,
and is marked *con anima*. It now literally soars
up the scale; we are carried irresistibly along,
the melody becoming more and more impassioned,
yet over all is that indefinable longing which it is
impossible to express in words. Once more the
question and its answer,—again a question, this
time a more emphatic reply mark the quintuplet
of crotchets, which a few bars further on we have
as a quadruplet. Once more the connecting quaver
phrases, and we are into the sublime melody again
emphasised the more by the lovely theme in C
sharp minor, by which it is followed,—a supplicating
theme as of a lover pleading at the feet of his
mistress. Now listen how coquettishly she replies,
how lightly she treats his avowal. Once more he
pleads in the same strain, even more coquettishly
does she answer. Now they are speaking rapidly

together, she with the clearness of stern resolve, he with the agitation of passionate uncertainty. Now she actually laughs in his face, such scornful laughter——. But we are wandering far a-field; would that we could follow him into the world of fancy and romance, the road to which he knew so well.

Such, however, is not our province, and we hasten to return to the calmer contemplation of the many beauties expressed in the music. After the light and delicate *arpeggi* a return is made in turn to the theme already heard, the work ending with the principal melody more expansively treated than before. Note the glorious effect of the transition through the key of F major in the last bars.

The No. 3, Op. 39 (composed during Chopin's sojourn in Majorca) perhaps justifies its title to a greater extent than its companions. It is certainly 'fitful,' if not exactly capricious. The contrast between the first part of the work with its *staccato*, and the following portion, which is almost of the character of a chorale, is effective. The chorale may be said to commence at the *meno mosso*, and to consist of sixteen bars; it is divided into four sections, and after each, and dividing one section from another, are four bars of quavers, *arpeggios*, lightly descending the scale from in *altissimo*. Gounod has employed a similar effect as regards the splitting up of the chorale in his church-scene in *Faust*; but in his case, after the broad *sostenuto* chords, he, instead of starting from the high pitch and descending, takes the note an octave below the last chord of the chorale, and builds upon it semiquavers in triplets, maintaining the same pitch throughout the bar. But this is only a difference of detail; the procedure is practically similar. The figure above mentioned and the *staccato* theme form the basis of this number.

The general atmosphere of the fourth and last of the Scherzos is much softer, and, if we may say so, more 'balmy' than in the preceding ones. There is a delicacy of subject and treatment alike, which does not exist in the others. The chief fault seems to lie in its inordinate length. Worthy of remark, perhaps, is the resemblance in tone of this Scherzo to the Ballade No. 3, Op. 47, though the similitude lies more in the musical thought than in its treatment. For example, a frequently recurring phrase in the Scherzo is :—

while in the Ballade we find this :—

Particularly worthy of notice is the harmonic progression which immediately follows the passage just quoted. Candidly speaking, I find this number more valuable for its exquisite treatment of detail than for its absolute originality of idea, although I am tempted to modify this statement on coming to the *più lento*. Here beauty reigns supreme, not for one moment allowing our attention to be centred on aught else but itself. On the return to the *tempo,*

I notice the fine effect attained by the opening phrase, accompanied by the double pedal, of which the dominant alternates with the note above as an auxiliary. Before closing our remarks upon this work, we wish to draw attention to the phrase of four bars immediately after the re-entry to the A flat key. It is certainly a modification of the opening phrase, but how much more mournful! Could anything be more suggestive of misery? Mark! we are discussing a 'Scherzo.' How wonderful is it, then, that we find the same theme in one of the latest masterpieces of modern music, and that masterpiece the Requiem Mass, Op. 89, of Antonin Dvorák! This identical theme we find in the opening bar of his work, and its use as a *motif*, expressive of the deepest sorrow, is continuous throughout. We mention this not merely as a thematic coincidence, but as a proof of how little the title of 'Scherzo' conveys the wonderful contrast of emotional power expressed in these tone-pictures. Also specially noticeable here is the masterly way in which we find Chopin handles his rhythm, which, although often unconventional, is never unsymmetrical.

CHAPTER VIII

ALTHOUGH of a peculiarly impressionable and susceptible disposition, and, as a not unnatural consequence, more or less fickle where women were concerned, Chopin's love affairs did, on more than one occasion, assume a serious aspect. We have already touched upon the episode of his early attachment to Constantia Gladkowska, to whom he referred in his letters as his 'Ideal.' But in his later letters to his friend Titus Woyciechowski, we find little or no mention of the lady. What was the immediate reason of this falling off in his ardour we do not know. Perhaps it was that he had learnt that his divinity had thoughts to bestow upon others than himself; and, if such were the case, it was quite sufficient in itself to account for the diminution of his affection for her. Such was his nature. It would have been utterly foreign to him to love for any length of time where he was not loved in return.

The slightest feeling not responded to chilled him at once. However, in 1832, Constantia Gladkowska married at Warsaw a merchant, Joseph Grabowski by name, whether for mercenary reasons or not we do not know; sufficient for us, that she forsook the less fortunate Frederic. Whether the wound thus inflicted was a deep one or not is also a matter upon which we can only conjecture; at all events, he had by now sufficiently recovered from its effects to find a fresh 'Ideal.' If we are guided to any extent by Madame Sand, we shall certainly not credit him with having any great depth of feeling or constancy; but before allowing ourselves to be influenced by her, we must always consider her proneness to exaggeration, and, moreover, her desire to depict Chopin in a light as unfavourable as possible. As illustrative of his fickleness, she relates the following story, which she asserts was told her by Chopin himself:—'He had conceived a fancy for the grand-daughter of a celebrated master, and, although contemplating matrimony with her, he had at the same time in his mind's eye another lady, resident in Poland; his loyalty being engaged nowhere, and his fickle heart concentrated on no one passion. One day, when visiting the former young lady in company with a musician, who was at the time better known in Paris than he himself, she unconsciously offered a chair to his companion first. So piqued was he at what he considered this slight, that he not only never called upon her again, but dismissed her entirely from his thoughts.' Were this story told by George Sand alone, we should, for the reasons above quoted, think twice before accepting it unreservedly; but it is corroborated by other and indisputable authorities, who could have no object in enlarging upon it, and we can only accept it as showing how really fickle was his disposition, and how small a thing it needed to waft him one way or the other. In the love affair with which we have now to deal, he found his 'Ideal' in the person of Maria Wodzinska. For particulars of it I have gone to Count Wodzinski's[1] *Trois Romans de Chopin*, which deals, as its title infers, almost entirely with the romantic episodes of his life. He tells us that the first meeting between Chopin

[1] In Polish family names ending with 'i,' the termination becomes 'a' when the name is applied to women.

and this lady took place during their childhood, he being ten and she five years of age. Maria was frequently at Nicholas Chopin's house with her mother, as her brothers were at that time residing with the Chopins. Thus an acquaintance sprung up, and Frederic, who was a frequent visitor at Sluzewo (the father's property), became an intimate friend of the family. It was, says the author of *Les Trois Romans*, these recollections alone which caused this new affection to spring up within him. After the Polish Revolution of 1830, the Wodzinskis moved to Geneva. There they remained until the year 1835, when they returned to Poland, breaking their journey at Dresden. Meanwhile Anthony Wodzinski, being in Paris, had kept Chopin well informed as to his family's movements.

In this same year, Nicholas Chopin was ordered by the doctors in Warsaw to take the waters at Carlsbad, and, as it was nearly five years since he had seen his father, Frederic determined to journey as far as that town and meet him. This he did, and, as it turned out, it was their last meeting. Having duly informed his father of his intentions with regard to Maria, he left for Dresden, where the Wodzinskis were staying. The young lady was now nineteen years of age, and is described as being of a tall, graceful figure, and having features which, although remarkable for neither regularity nor classic beauty, had an indefinite charm. Her magnificent hair, we read, was silky, and black as ebony, her nose being somewhat pronounced, and her whole face highly intelligent. For a month the two now met constantly at the house of her uncle, the Palatine Wodzinski, making music together, and passing the evenings in one another's company. Chopin, whilst now once again a victim to the tender passion, composed the Waltz (No. 1 of Op. 69), the MS.—a copy of which appears in Count Wodzinski's book—bearing in the right-hand corner the words, ' Pour Mlle. Marie,' and the subscription, ' F. Chopin, Dresden, September 1835.' Up to now Chopin had made no direct avowal, and did not do so until they met again in the course of the following summer at Marienbad.

As to the lady's reply to his proposal, his several biographers are once more at variance. Karasowski relates that 'Chopin soon discovered that Maria reciprocated his affection, and that they were formally engaged with the consent and approval of their relatives'; whilst, on the other hand, the author of *Les Trois Romans* tells us that her reply was to the effect that she could not act in opposition to her parents' wishes, which she could not hope to alter, but that she would always preserve for him in her heart a grateful remembrance.' This reply is characteristic, and bears the impress of truth, inasmuch as it is but a slight variation of that so often resorted to by the fair sex under similar circumstances, when they express a desire to be allowed to act the part of a sister towards the unfortunate suitor. But of these two contradictory statements we are inclined to take this latter as the correct one, for, besides being a relative of the lady, Count Wodzinski asserts that at a later period of her life she herself told him of her reply to Chopin's proposal. The only way, therefore, in which it could be unreliable would be in the event of Miss Maria wishing to do away with any impression which might exist that she had engaged herself to and finally jilted her lover. She may have felt that her action in marrying during the following year a son of Chopin's godfather, Count Frederic Skarbek, had given rise to such an assumption. But even if that were so, we can only give her the benefit of the doubt. Moreover, supposing she did behave thoughtlessly,—if not heartlessly,—she was sufficiently punished by the result of her marriage, which was a most unhappy one, and had finally to be dissolved.

Not less unreliable is the statement of Karasowski, that Chopin intended to marry and withdraw himself from the world, and to settle near his family in Warsaw, and there to establish a school for the people; while he, without troubling himself about the public, quietly pursued his art. Apart from the unlikelihood of his selecting such a life, how could he have contemplated such a course on what we know were his resources at this time? Assuredly, so long as he remained in Paris, he could by teaching make a good income; but he had been so short a time even in this position, that it was quite impossible he could have saved sufficient to enable him to support his wife and himself, not to mention any indulgence in philanthropic schemes. We can only assume that his biographer means that his wife would bring him a fortune. But here, again, he is in error, for although of an aristocratic and wealthy family, she was not to become possessed of her fortune until after the death of her parents.

On leaving Marienbad, Chopin once more turned his steps towards Leipzig. Of his meeting here with Robert Schumann we have direct testimony in the form of a letter from the latter musician to Heinrich Dorn, in which he says:—'The day before yesterday, just after I had received your letter, and was about to answer it, who should enter? Chopin. This was to me a great pleasure. We passed a very happy day together, in honour of which I made yesterday a holiday. . . . He played, in addition to a number of Etudes, several Nocturnes and Mazurkas—everything incomparable. You would like him immensely.' Here, also, is direct evidence of the very high opinion held by Schumann, not only of Chopin himself, but of his works.

Having thus pleasantly broken the journey at

Leipzig, Chopin continued his way homeward *via*
Heidelberg. This brings us to the end of the
year 1836. The year following was to be one
of great moment for Chopin, for in it occurred
the episode which has done much to colour his
life from this time. We refer to his meeting with
George Sand. With this important event it is our
intention to deal in the next chapter, but in the
meantime it will, perhaps, be of interest if we form
a preliminary acquaintance with the heroine of what
has been termed the greatest 'romance' of Chopin's
life. Madame Sand,—we should say Mademoiselle
Aurore Dupin,—was born some five years earlier than
Frederic Chopin. Her father, Maurice Dupin—an
officer in the army, and the grandson of the Maré-
chal de Saxe—had fallen in love with, and finally
married, the daughter of a Parisian bird-seller, by
name Sophie Delaborde. That the mother of
Maurice Dupin was opposed to the match does not
surprise us, when we consider the difference in
social status existing between the contracting parties.
Nevertheless, the old lady's prejudices were in some
degree overcome, when, on the birth of their daughter,

M. and Madame Dupin placed their offspring under the care of its grandmother. Four years later Maurice Dupin died at his mother's country seat— Nohant. The infant daughter now became the cause of increased wrangling between its mother and grandmother, who, it may be imagined, had never been on any terms of marked friendliness. At the age of thirteen Aurore was sent to a convent, where she appears to have earned for herself the character of ringleader where any kind of mischief was concerned. But her precocity in this undesirable direction did not last long; for, proceeding to the other extreme, she became nothing short of a victim to religious mania, and seriously (if we can regard her intentions then as in any way deserving of that title) thought of taking the veil, and devoting herself to a life of religious seclusion. This, however, by the intervention of her half-brother, was prevented, not so much by force of persuasion on his part, as by initiating the young lady in such healthy exercises and pleasures as the country house at Nohant naturally afforded. At seventeen years of age, be it said to her credit, she began to awaken to the fact that it was time she set about the improvement of those mental qualities which she possessed—as was afterwards proved—in so great a degree.

Thomas à Kempis's *Imitation of Christ*, to which she had hitherto gone for religious sustenance, was no longer sufficient for the accomplishment of her more ambitious and more worldly desires. Therefore we find her devoting her attention to the works of such writers as Chateaubriand, Bacon, Milton, and Shakespeare. This, undoubtedly, had its effect. Through the death of her grandmother, she now inherited a considerable fortune, and had she been willing to desert her mother for the aristocratic relations of her father, they would, no doubt, have been willing to accord her their patronage and protection. But this she would not do. She was now eighteen years of age, and young as she was, she married Casimir Dudevant, a young man some nine years her senior, who, after serving in the army as a lieutenant, had relinquished his military career in quest of forensic honours.

Young as they were, their marriage does not

seem to have been one of even ordinary romantic surroundings. On the contrary, it would seem to have had for its basis 'a lasting friendship,' for the novelist herself tells us that her would-be husband spoke little to her of love; being nothing if not matter-of-fact. The result cannot be said to have been satisfactory. The 'friendship' on which they had so depended for their happiness was not, at all events, sufficiently strong to compensate for the differences in their respective temperaments. Moreover, her brother Hippolyte made matters considerably worse for her, for in addition to so mismanaging her business affairs as to leave her almost without means of any kind, he led the husband into intemperate habits, and so widened the breach already existing between them as to render a separation absolutely necessary. Thus it is that we find Madame Dudevant on her own account in Paris, endeavouring in literature to find a means of support.

The conditions of her separation were, that in addition to her daughter, Solange, being allowed to pass three months in the year with her, she was to receive from her husband an allowance of 250 francs per month. On this she established herself in three rooms in a Mansarde on the Quai Saint Michel, doing most of the household work herself. Her literary career began from this time; and she devoted herself entirely to the study of man and his manners. Her first work, *Rose et Blanche*, produced in 1831, was so great a success that she was commissioned by the publishers to follow it up with another. The first novel had been written in collaboration with Jules Sandeau, but the second, *Indiana*, was her own work entirely. We must not omit to mention that, as a result of this collaboration, the initial book was published under the *nom de plume* of Jules Sand. Consequently on its success, she was desirous of adhering to this name; but as Jules Sandeau had had no part in the second work, he objected. The publishers were naturally anxious to retain the name, and finally a compromise was suggested by them; this was, that she should alter the name to Georges Sand. To this name she adhered, and, as we know, made it famous throughout the civilised world.

Her financial position was now considerably amelior-
ated. The two novels, although not bringing her any
very large sum, realised the useful amount of £120.
Her literary career from this time was one of steady
progress.   In the year following the publication of
Indiana, she made the acquaintance of Alfred de
Musset.

Of the *liaison* which was the outcome of this
acquaintance it is not within our province here
to speak, further than the recording of it.   During this time the disagreements between Mme.
Dudevant and her husband in no wise dimin-
ished, she complaining chiefly on the score that
her financial position was inadequate.   In her favour,
it must be remembered, that her husband had, from
the beginning, lived upon her, his only expectations
being, that he would receive money on the death of
his stepmother.   Frequent arrangements were made
between them, only to be broken, and in the end Mme.
Dudevant applied for a judicial separation, which the
court duly granted to her.   Her husband appealed,
but withdrew before judgment was given.   As is invariably the case in these matters, there is much to

be said on both sides, but however lenient we may be disposed to be towards the woman who so worthily added to the literary art of her country, one cannot deny the fact that she was of a nature the reverse of admirable,—a woman who, while stopping at nothing in the gratification of her desires, yet was ever ready with an excuse for herself, and who *posed* before the world as an example of all that was good and upright in womanhood. Moreover, she seems to have been wanting alike in tact, reserve, and dignity of conduct; while by no means the least noticeable feature in her character was the manner in which she succeeded in deceiving even herself.

But as we have now sufficiently fulfilled our object, which has been, by giving the reader some idea of her parentage and surroundings, to aid him in forming some slight idea of the woman with whom so much of Chopin's life, from this time forth, was spent, we may continue our perusal of the master's works.

The group upon which we shall now direct our attention is that which contains four compositions under the title of 'Ballades.' These are severally, the Op. 23 in G minor, dedicated to Baron

Stockhausen, and published in June 1836; Op. 38 in F minor, dedicated to Robert Schumann, and published in 1840; Op. 47 in A flat major, dedicated to Mlle. de Noailles, published in 1841, and Op. 52 in F major, dedicated to the Baroness de Rothschild, and published in 1843. These four compositions, the form and title of which, Schumann tells us, were originally inspired by the poems of the Polish bard Mickiewicz, represent the most masterly and powerful efforts of Chopin's genius. The first, in G minor, opens with seven introductory bars in common time, more or less forming an opening recitative. About the last chord of this introduction there has been considerable controversy.

In some editions it is terminated, as in the accompanying example, with a dissonant E flat.* This,

according to the testimony of his pupils Gutmann

and Mikuli, is what Chopin intended. On the other
hand, Klindworth, although adhering to it in his
edition, explained that he found it in an English
edition, and that his only reason for retaining it was,
that he liked the effect. Xaver Scharwenka, who
revised the Klindworth edition for Messrs. Augener,
states, in a footnote, that, as there is no doubt that
D was the note intended, he has thus altered it.
But while we cannot but accept the testimony of the
two pupils named above, the effect of the E flat as
written is so harsh, that we infinitely prefer the
passage as Scharwenka has altered it. Nevertheless,
we cannot help feeling that what Chopin really
intended was, so far as concerns the E flat in the
chord, an effect similar to that in the following cadence, which we get twenty-eight bars later.

But the matter is at most a small one. After these

introductory bars the 'story' commences, and is told us in a beautifully undulating melody in ⁶⁄₄ time, the rhythm of which is no less charming in its originality. At the *a tempo* following the cadence just quoted the music becomes more animated, four bars later developing into *agitato*, and continues to increase in vigour until we reach the *poco a poco meno forte*, from whence it dies away until the *meno mosso* movement is reached. Here an entirely new theme is presented,—perhaps the most beautiful in the work. No words can convey the delicious languor of which it is redolent. Notice especially here, and indeed throughout the Ballade, the frequent use of the chord of the thirteenth. Some twenty-four bars later the initial theme makes its re-appearance in the key of A minor, but on this occasion the two unaccented beats in the left hand retain the dominant pedal throughout, greatly lending to the effect of the long and passionate *crescendo* which is to come a few bars further on, and at the climax of which we are plunged into the *meno mosso* theme, *ff*. This theme here reappears in a very different guise, both it and its accompaniment being harmonically varied and strengthened. As we proceed the music becomes more and more impassioned, a climax being reached at the *ffz*, after which we get a lull. But this does not continue for long, for the quaver notes gradually ascend the scale, and insinuatingly wind themselves into an undulating chain of melody, such as no other composer knew how to weave. After a further modified presentment of the *meno mosso* phrase, followed in its turn by a re-appearance of the initial theme, the work is brought to a conclusion by some fifty-six bars of *presto con fuoco*. In this short section wildness reigns supreme, the last part consisting of a seething mass of chromatics and octaves, the latter now in contrary, now in similar, motion, until after a final semi-tonic rush we are landed almost breathless on the tonic chord.

When we consider the unconventionality and the amount of originality contained in the work, we cannot much wonder at its appearance having been the signal for an onslaught on the part of many of the musical critics of the time. It altogether passed their understanding. They were no more able to recognise the dramatic element contained in it than they were competent to appreciate its many details and technical beauties. Schumann referred to it as Chopin's *genialischtes* work, and was more partial to it than to either of its companions. / Looked at as music *per se*, I do not think the second Ballade can compare with the first. The opening *andantino*, in its elegant simplicity, undoubtedly charms, but it is with difficulty that we can get over the lack of affinity of the *presto con fuoco* with this preceding section. By far the most interesting portion is at the first return of the first movement, where the composer indulges in thematic treatment of its subject. The re-appearance of the *presto* takes us on to an *agitato coda* in A minor. But this is not concluded without once more bringing before us a modification of the initial phrase. With this in the A minor key the Ballade closes, and although no less fantastic, yet it is indubitably inferior to its predecessor as regards its æsthetic effect.

We now come to No. 3, in which we have the composer in quite a different mood. The whole atmosphere of this piece is playful and delicate, and forms a vivid contrast with any of its companions. The similarity between the opening phrase of this work and a portion of the Scherzo 3, Op. 54, we have already touched upon. The opening four bars contain a complete question and answer, while the syncopations which follow are essentially characteristic of the whole Ballade throughout which they are maintained. Especially is this so with the lovely theme in F major, one of the most delicate and idealistic to be found even amongst the many idealities he has given us. This Ballade breathes nothing but Chopin. Whose spirit but his is present in those finely undulating semiquaver figures, those 'essential' harmonies, those wonderfully artistic cogitations on the thematic material, the hundred and one little evidences of a keen perception of the refined in art. Look at the section in C sharp minor, and notice the inverted dominant pedal in the right hand while the left is carrying on the theme. We can imagine the master's care in the interpretation of such a passage which, without the requisite art and feeling in the performer, would instantly become commonplace. Yet, in addition to all this, the hand of the master who can handle the more 'robust' in his art is equally evident in the concluding portion, the harmonic grandeur of which cannot but impress us, and which forms so effective a conclusion to the *spirituelle* which has preceded it. The chief fault to be found with the fourth and last Ballade is that a certain monotony is felt by the somewhat excessive use of the original theme. It is presented to us in various ways, each individually beautiful; yet, taken as a whole, it seems to lack that contrast and *esprit* which is so conspicuous a feature of its companions. Nevertheless it is very lovely. Specially would we point out the eighteen bars which occur in the middle of the work, marked *a tempo primo*, and which entirely defy any such thing as cold criticism. The devotional spirit which they breathe is unmistakable, and if we descend to technical comment it is only to point out one transition more supremely beautiful than the rest.

Later on towards the close of the work, at the *stretto*, we have a very fine harmonic progression, but space prevents us from quoting this and many other details over which we would fain linger. In conclusion, although their number is so small, it is in these four Ballades that is noticeable the composer's method more than in any of the others. Those thoughts which were nipped in the bud by such fetters as those imposed by, for instance, the Sonata form, here flourish in all their luxuriance. Here the composer, feeling himself untrammelled, gives his fancy free rein. Sad and happy thoughts chase one another incessantly. His thoughts ended, his work is ended. It is essentially ' programme ' music, founded upon definite creations of the composer's brain, and expressed now in the most idealistic and now in the most realistic manner by him.

CHAPTER IX

On Robert Schumann's very high opinion of Chopin's work we touched in the last chapter. That one artist should hold and express such opinions of another was, even in those days, remarkable; but not only did Schumann feel with regard to Chopin's works, what no artist could help feeling, namely, their great value as the expression of original genius, but he did not hesitate to express publicly his opinion, and that without qualification in the smallest degree; and there is no doubt that, had Schumann refrained from so doing, the fame of Chopin, in Germany at all events, would have taken a much longer time to spread. As it was, owing to the attention drawn towards his works by Schumann, his works were at this time the topic of much discussion amongst musicians in that country. And if a work be artistic, original, and thorough, discussion amongst the enlightened may be said to be the stepping-stone to acceptance. It is, therefore, with the greater regret on this account that we find that Chopin did not reciprocate this feeling of admiration for the work of a fellow-artist, especially when that artist was a musician of so much originality of thought as Robert Schumann. Had it been a musician whose theory was the absolute sacrifice of thought to form, it would have been the more easy to understand, but in the case of Schumann, who at that time revealed so much of the beautiful in his work, it is inexplicable. When one has regard to the prominent qualities which may be said in a sense, to obtrude from the work of different musicians, it does seem curious that Chopin should have admired a musician such as Bellini (whom he undoubtedly did admire), and have, practically speaking, expressed his contempt for a musician such as was Robert Schumann ; that he did do this we know on the authority of one of his most famous pupils, M. Mathias.[1]   He relates that on one occasion Schumann sent S. Heller a copy of his *Carnaval,*

---

[1] Niecks's *Life of Chopin.*

the Opus 9, which had just been published, to present to Chopin. It was luxuriously bound, and the title-page printed in colours. Heller called on the Polish musician in order to carry out his commission, and handed him the music; and after having examined it, Chopin merely remarked, 'How beautifully they get up these things in Germany.' He could not have been more severe had he been speaking of some purveyor of sentimental drawing-room songs, who, recognising the inability of his notes to convey anything but confusion, was obliged to have recourse to the artist and his colour-box. One can understand his antipathy to the compositions of Liszt, for never was barrenness of idea more exemplified than in those works of the great pianist which he has been pleased to call original compositions. As an adapter of other men's ideas, written for other instruments, to his own instrument, he has never been equalled and can never be excelled, particularly as regards the arrangement of orchestral music for the piano. His manner of transforming figures which, in the orchestral score, appear the very antithesis of pianoforte music, into figures which are not only eminently suitable, but frequently the most effective parts of the work when played upon the pianoforte, amounts almost in itself to genius; and had his power in composing and handling original melodies been on a par with his great talent in the direction we have just mentioned, there is no doubt they would have been great works. But, unhappily, such was by no means the case, and Liszt's works were never favourably looked upon by Chopin. Neither did he admire Berlioz, nor even Meyerbeer. The composers for whose works he seems to have shown preference, at all events as regards giving them to his pupils for study, were : — Schubert, Mozart, Beethoven, Bach, Handel, Dussek, and Field.

It is now time that we touch upon an incident in the life of our artist, to which we referred in the last chapter, and about which much has been written— some of it true, most of it, unfortunately, untrue and highly coloured. We do not wish to deny that Chopin's connection with Madame Aurora Dudevant (George Sand) is of great importance. It undoubtedly was, and did much to influence a certain period of his life. But the art of fiction should trespass no more on that of biography than the biographer should have recourse to fiction in relating any incident in the life of the person of whom he may be writing. As we have before said, of all famous men Chopin has, perhaps, been the one most sinned against in this matter. Everyday commonplaces in his life have been turned and twisted into fulsome romances, more or less coloured according to the talent of the writer in that direction. It has been our purpose, in this necessarily short biography, to state nothing for which chapter and verse has not been, or cannot be, found. Nor do we propose to go very minutely into the details of his connection with George Sand, but to speak of it only so far as it affects the life and character of our artist. Those who would read the graphic descriptions we speak of can have no difficulty in finding them, as their name is legion amongst the biographies of Chopin. Therefore we will simply state, without embellishment of any kind, that Chopin met George Sand under circumstances which are so absolutely ordinary as to not even give the most imaginative reader scope for exercise of his imagination. One of the vices of George Sand seems to have been not an extraordinary one in women generally: that of curiosity. This fatal feeling had been aroused by the accounts she had heard of Chopin and of his compositions. She therefore asked a mutual friend, Franz Liszt, to introduce Chopin to her. Liszt, of course, said he would do so, and accordingly spoke to Chopin about it. Chopin, however, did not seem at all anxious on his part to make the acquaintance of a 'literary woman.' Whether he had any definite reason for this we are not told. At all events one can perhaps in some measure understand his prejudices. But either the curiosity aroused in the person of George Sand was phenomenally great, or it was not curiosity alone which prompted her in the matter, for she carried the day and was introduced by Liszt to Chopin in his own rooms, on the occasion of a small party given by Chopin to a few musical intimates, for the purpose of playing to them some new works which he had recently completed. It may be well to say *en passant* that the meeting has been generally described as having taken place at a soirée given by Madame la Comtesse d'Agoult at the Hotel de France. The mistake has probably arisen in this wise: The Comtesse d'Agoult was a very intimate friend of Liszt, and George Sand herself says in her *Histoire* that she first met Chopin through Madame d'Agoult. As Madame d'Agoult (known in the literary world as Daniel Stern) accompanied Liszt and Madame Sand to Chopin's rooms, it is not unnatural that Madame d'Agoult's name should have been associated with their first meeting. Besides, George Sand does not say that it was Chopin alone whom she met through her friend, but mentions his name in conjunction with Eugene Sue, Mickiewicz the poet, Nourrit the singer, and others. It is true that she afterwards met Chopin at one of the soirées given by the Comtesse d'Agoult.

The first impression made by the novelist upon Chopin does not seem to have been a favourable one. This is not to be wondered at, seeing that, both as regards appearance and character, George Sand was quite the reverse of Chopin; for we can take A. de Musset's description of her at the time it was made,— which was after he had first made her acquaintance,— as being reliable.

He describes her as 'brown, pale, dull-complexioned, with reflections as of bronze, and strikingly large-eyed like an Indian,' while Heine describes her as having a face beautiful rather than interesting, her features being almost Grecian in their regularity. A mobile face certainly, with low forehead, and eyes the reverse from bright, though he says 'her bodily frame seems to be somewhat too stout and too short. She appears to have had an extraordinary power of fascination, and to have exercised it upon Chopin to such an extent that, in a short time, he was her devoted slave. May be that his disappointment in connection with his former love, Maria Wodzinska, had rendered him the more easy captive to her fascinations; but be that as it may, it rendered his subjugation to the strong and dominating passion of Madame Sand none the less lasting.

The meeting we have above described took place in the early part of the year 1837, and in the summer of this same year Chopin made his first visit to our metropolis. Accompanied by Pleyel, the pianoforte manufacturer and publisher, he arrived in

London on the 11th July, and remained for some ten days. It appears Pleyel introduced him to James Broadwood as M. Fritz! With what reason, unless it were a joke, we do not know; however, the pseudonym was soon discovered. Although he only played in private, he excited the almost universal admiration of all the competent critics who had the good fortune to hear him. Mr. J. W. Davison, then critic of the recently defunct *Musical World*, wrote an especially eulogistic account of his performances in that journal. On his return to Paris his health gave him serious cause for anxiety, and as decided evidences of chest complaint showed themselves, he remained in Paris, seeing a great deal, the while, of George Sand, and the following winter, at her invitation, he decided to accompany her party to the South of France, whither she was going, chiefly for the sake of her son's health. Thither Madame Sand and her family set out in November 1838, Chopin arranging to join them at Perpignan. Although in very delicate health, he was for the moment considerably stronger than he had been for some time past, and bore the fatigue of the journey much better than his friends had anticipated. Palma was their destination, travelling by way of Port Vendres and Barcelona. For the sea voyages they were favoured with fine weather, and, after having left Paris a fortnight previous in bitterly cold weather, arrived in Palma under a glorious sun, and found, in the words of the novelist herself, 'a green Switzerland under a Calabrian sky, with all the solemnity and stillness of the East.' 'The country, nature, trees, sky, sea and mountains surpass all my dreams,' she writes the first few days after their arrival; 'it is the promised land, and we are delighted.' But, like many places, the beauties of which our novelists never tire of depicting, the realisation, so far as regards submitting to the corresponding discomforts and inconveniences, falls far short of the description. Even to-day one's own experience teaches that it is much better to read our novelist's graphic and vivid depictions of any of those places which lie out of the beaten track, than to attempt to experience the delights they so beautifully describe. Even more so was it then, as our party found to their cost in a very short time. There appears to have been no hotel there whatever, and they were obliged to be content with the only lodging they could procure, which consisted of two very small rooms, very poorly furnished,—in fact, from the account Madame Sand gives of them, they could not be termed furnished in any proper sense of the word. Happily, they were not doomed to remain in these quarters for long, as in the neighbourhood they chanced to find an empty villa, which they did not hesitate to procure. Rent, 50 francs a month. This villa, appropriately named the Villa Son-Vent, they made their residence, until they were compelled to leave by bad weather. Truly it was named a 'House of the Wind' and rain, and it fully acted up to its title:—'The walls of it were so thin that the lime with which our rooms were plastered swelled like a sponge. For us, who were accustomed to warm ourselves in cold weather, this house without a chimney was like a mantle of ice upon our shoulders, and I felt paralysed. Our invalid began to ail and cough, and from this moment we became an object of dread and horror to the people. We were accused and convicted of pulmonary phthisis,

which is equivalent to the plague in the prejudices regarding contagion entertained by Spanish
physicians.' So writes Mme. Sand in her *Hiver
à Majorque.* It therefore became necessary for the
party once 'more to look about them for a more
habitable dwelling. This, after much trouble, they
found in the Carthusian monastery of Valdemosa,
where at the time were hidden a Spanish refugee
and his wife. The couple, being anxious to leave
the island at once, gladly grasped the opportunity
held out to them, and disposed of their cell and
furniture to George Sand for the sum of a thousand
francs. For a faithful description of their abode,
which is so interesting to the Chopin-lover as being
the place wherein he wrote much of his most
beautiful work, we cannot do better than quote
from Mr. Wood's delightful series of *Letters from
Majorca.*[1] Speaking of the Carthusian monastery,
he says: 'In the winter we had not visited the
monastery. We did so to-day. I especially wished
to make its acquaintance. For me it bore a name-

---

[1] *Letters from Majorca,* by Charles W. Wood, F.R.G.S.
London: R. Bentley and Sons, 1888.

less charm.   It was here that, fifty years ago,
George Sand had spent a winter, accompanied by
her children and by Chopin.   Imagine a man of
Chopin's delicate health and sensitive temperament
spending a winter in Mallorca.   It was a season of
snow and frost, too, as George Sand has recorded.
Even to-day, in visiting the island, you have to rough
it to some extent; but fifty years ago the life here
for a stranger was almost aboriginal.   No one wanted
him.   He was a spy upon the land, like Caleb and
Joshua: an intruder, who was sent to Coventry.   It
nearly cost Chopin his life, and no doubt hastened
his end. . . . We first entered the church attached
to the monastery, an empty building, of fine propor-
tions, dimly lighted.   Our footsteps echoed under
the vaulted roof.   At the farther end, behind a
screen, was a harmonium. . . . An opposite door led
into the cloisters,—ancient, substantial, picturesque,
beginning to crumble. . . . They form a small, perfect
quadrangle.   Running out, and away from these
cloisters, are long, very long corridors, with vaulted
roofs.   At the end, looking quite mysterious, and
far off and poetical, like a distant star, a lantern

or rose window admits a little light upon the scene. On one side of the corridor, large square windows permit a little sunshine to enter, and throw deep lights and shadows upon walls and pavement. Opposite the windows are the doors of the cells. We were admitted to one of them this morning, as, for the time being, it was untenanted. Each block consists of several rooms, large and lofty.'

Of George Sand's particular apartment, he says: 'Her apartment was the very last in the corridor, close to the rose window. Here they spent months of misery and privation; were nearly starved to death: almost perished in the cold of that unusually severe winter. It was impossible to warm these great rooms. People would not wait upon them. It was difficult to obtain fuel. They were treated as heathens by the priest-ridden, superstitious race, because George Sand, on her first appearance, had failed to attend mass. And, as the mischief was done, she never went to church at all. With the Mallorcans such a thing as atonement found no place. So for this neglect they were persecuted. Of course, they ought never to have gone there.'

Having thus (we will not say comfortably) established our artist in his monastery, we will proceed to discuss the result, musically speaking, of his sojourn there, so far, at all events, as regards the collection of short pieces, entitled *Préludes*, Op. 28, of which there are twenty-four, and one, Op. 45, published separately. Strictly speaking, the Prelude is understood to be the introduction to a fugue or chorale, such as Sebastian Bach has given us; indeed, he may be said to have gone so far as to have written some of his Preludes more in the character of a *toccata* than in any other. Therefore it is essential, in looking at these compositions (if such they may be called) of Chopin, that we dismiss this meaning of the word from our minds, and simply look at them as the pure essence of the composer's musical thoughts at the time—one might say the vivid reflection of his inner self. And although we are taking them as the direct result of his stay in Valdemosa, it is an open question whether they were all actually conceived by him at that time. George Sand not only states that they were, but gives us some highly-coloured pictures and anecdotes in connection with the creation of some of them. Gutmann, the favourite pupil of Chopin, distinctly avers that he saw the original MSS. before Chopin left Paris; but, although I am inclined to agree with Professor Niecks's reasoning, that the early Opus number indicates the existence of some of them prior to this time, yet they are so varied in character that I think there can be no doubt that certain of them, such as Nos. 4, 6, 9, 13, 20, and 21, were written at Valdemosa, and that Chopin, having sketches of others by him, completed the whole there, and published them under one Opus number. The atmosphere of those which I have named is morbid and azotic; to them there clings a faint flavour of disease, a something which is over-ripe in its lusciousness and febrile in its passion. This, in itself, inclines me to believe that they were written at the time we have named. As it would encroach too much upon the space at our command to examine each of these Preludes carefully, we must, perforce, rest content with a glance at the salient points of those we select. No. 2, with its discordant quaver figure, is morbid in the extreme. Note the Chopinesque phrase in this number,—

and compare it with bar 25 of the Nocturne No. 1, Op. 9, where we find it written thus,—

although the harmonic treatment of the phrase varies considerably. The flowing semiquaver figure of the accompaniment in No. 3 is essentially French. This figure is adhered to throughout the number, but the melody is not remarkable. It is difficult to find an adjective to fully express the exquisite sadness of No. 4, one of the most beautiful of these spontaneous sketches; for they are no more than sketches. The melody seems literally to wail, and reaches its greatest pitch of intensity at the *stretto.* It is with a sigh of relief that we come upon No. 5; a charming allegro movement in D major. But it is only to be plunged once more into the prostration of soul expressed in the next Prelude in B minor. In No. 9 we have perhaps some of the 'broadest' writing the composer has given us; short as it is, there is a majestic air about it, such as we do not often find him giving expression to. It might almost be termed 'Schumannish,' yet the individuality of its creator is over it all. Of No. 11, no one who hears the first four bars could help exclaiming that is 'Chopin.' On reaching No. 13 one is inclined to be invidious, and to exclaim 'here is the most beautiful of all.' Indeed, I think, were I asked to make selection I should choose Nos. 13 and 15. Notice specially in No. 13 the rare beauty of the *più lento* portion, and the original manner of ending the work. Indeed, throughout all his work his originality in closing is remarkable. He never, like many other composers, spoils his previous effort by a commonplace or tedious ending. All is as easy and natural as it is removed from the ordinary. No. 15 opens with melody at once pathetic and sweet; sadness seems to be more emphatically expressed in bars eleven and twelve. In reference to this special Prelude I will quote from George Sand's *Histoire* once again. 'While staying in this "card-house" he composed some short but very beautiful pieces, which he modestly entitled "Preludes"; they were real master-pieces. Some of them create such vivid impressions that the shades of the dead monks seem to rise and pass before the hearer in solemn and gloomy funereal pomp.' Nothing could be more descriptive than this of the middle section of the Prelude 15 in D flat. A marked feature of the work is the almost continuous use of the dominant pedal throughout. All through the first section, whilst we are in D flat, we have the reiteration of the quaver note, and after reaching the change to C sharp minor we find it even more marked; as an inverted pedal the G sharp alone being played by the right hand, while the left plays the stately four crotchet chords to the bar which gives us the idea so graphically described by George Sand. Twelve bars after the 'entry' to C sharp minor we are in E major, and here we get the continuous beat of the dominant again, this time in octaves, the melody in the bass being also strengthened by the addition of an inner part. Once more we are in C sharp minor, and the same section is repeated; the melody now occurs in the upper part in octaves, the pedal accompanying note having receded into the second part; four bars later the octaves give way to three-part chords, and the accompanying pedal note takes the tenor part, and so we are led on until, at the re-entry of the key of D flat we have the G sharp enharmonically changed to the A flat, and do not cease to hear its incessant beat until after six bars, when perhaps the most marvellous effect of the whole work is reached, and all is quiet, save the supplicating phrase of the melody—

the first note of which is forte, with a *diminuendo* as we descend the scale. Then, once more, the incessant beat of the pedal note for six bars, the last two of which are marked *ritenuto.*

None but a genius could have led us through this

without causing monotony. But no description in words can give us the true idea of its absolute beauty, its poetry, and its refinement. It is Chopin himself, and Chopin at his best. When we say this we say everything. Having lingered in one sense somewhat unduly, though in another insufficiently, over this number, we can only glance at Nos. 20 and 21 before proceeding with the life of the composer. Some twelve bars only go to make up No. 20. It is merely a sketch in bold colours with a wealth of music. The melody is responsive in character, and the modulation very beautiful, yet withal quite easy. It was evidently conceived much in the same spirit as Schumann's *Nachtstück*, No. 1, Op. 23, with which a comparison is interesting.

At the commencement of No. 21 we are struck with the daintiness of the diverging quaver figure of accompaniment. After the first sixteen bars we come to a melody similar in character to that in the last ten bars of No. 13. And although the quaver figure in its first form is dropped here, the composer takes it up again sixteen bars later in both hands, weaving above it his melody with a strong accent on the first beat of the bar, while the quaver figure fills up the remainder. We now lose sight of it again in the form, though it is there in the spirit, up to the last bar. No. 24 is intensely Chopinesque, and with it we are brought to the end of the Opus, and it is not without regret that we leave these reflections of the composer's mind, which contain such an inexhaustible wealth of melody, poetry, and passion.

CHAPTER X

Notwithstanding the considerable trouble and inconvenience through which they had passed, life in the ex-monastery seems for a time to have held considerable charm for Madame Sand and her children. In addition to the furniture procured from the Spanish couple, they had been able to purchase more accessories with which to make themselves comfortable, and altogether things were a great improvement upon what they had been. But all this time our poor Chopin was without his piano. He had sent for one to Pleyel of Paris, his favourite maker; but it took some two months to effect its transit, and when it did arrive he was compelled to pay customs duty upon it to the amount of some 300 francs. Their life was necessarily an extremely quiet and simple one. In the morning George Sand occupied herself with giving lessons to her children, the afternoon being devoted to her literary work whilst the children were out, Chopin devoting himself to improvising, and composing mainly in the evenings. The chief difficulty experienced was in procuring sufficiently strengthening diet for the invalid, for although Madame Sand's son Maurice had greatly benefited by the change, such was not the case with Chopin. In the weak state of health in which he then was it was essential that he should have nutritious food; whereas the only thing they could be at all sure of procuring was pork. Such fowls as they were able to get were so poor as to be not worth the cooking, and it is terrible to think of what straits they might have been put to had it not been for the assistance of the French consul's cook, who, whenever the weather permitted, sent them over provisions. Surely life under such circumstances was the last thing in the world to which a man suffering from a lung complaint should have been subjected, to say nothing of the fact that he was of most refined tastes, and almost inclined to be epicurean with regard to his food. Besides this, Chopin appears to have been much depressed by the very scenery amid which they

had taken up their residence. No one who has not
lived for a considerable time amongst them can have
an adequate idea of the deep gloom cast on all around
by olive trees. At first sight they are, by reason of
the very quality which afterwards makes them
monotonous, very beautiful to the eye. Together
with this all the surroundings were decidedly
depressing; witness George Sand's description of the
place:—'I never heard the wind sound so much like
mournful voices and give forth such despairing howls
as in these empty and sonorous galleries. The
noise of the torrents, the swift motion of the clouds,
the grand monotonous sound of the sea, interrupted
by the whistling of the storm and the plaintive cries
of the sea birds which passed quite terrified and
bewildered in the squalls, then thick fogs which fell
suddenly like a shroud, and which, penetrating into
the cloisters through the broken arcades, rendered us
invisible . . . all combined made indeed this monastery the most romantic abode in the world.'

The 'romantic' element referred to does not seem
to have been able to hold out against the counteract-
ing element of desolation, for shortly after writing the

above she says :—'As the winter advanced sadness more and more paralysed my efforts at gaiety and cheerfulness. The state of our invalid grew worse and worse, the wind howled in the ravines, the rain beat against our windows, the voice of the thunder penetrated through our thick walls, and mingled its mournful sounds with the laughter and play of the children. . . . The raging sea kept the ships in the harbours; we felt ourselves prisoners far from all enlightened help and from sympathy. Death seemed to hover over our heads to seize one of us, and we were alone in contending with him for his prey.' Truly a dispiriting picture, and if dispiriting to the vivacious novelist in good health, how much more so to the delicate musician, accustomed only to the bright salons of Parisian society. No wonder that his one desire was to return to Paris. The damp and bad weather had had their injurious effect upon him, and it now became a question as to whether he would be able to move for some time. Neither does Madame Sand seem to have escaped the fatal influences of their discomfort, she having suffered severely from rheumatism. While in the monastery she completed

her novel of monastic life—*Spiridion*, and no doubt
for this purpose she could not have lived in a more
suitable place. Apart from even the climatic hard-
ships, they found it next to impossible to procure any
servants, and even the maid whom Madame Sand had
brought from France, at an enormous wage, began to
refuse attendance, saying the work and discomforts
were too much for her.

Much of the novelist's time was now taken up in
nursing the invalid, as of all things he disliked
being left alone. Moreover, as time went on he
grew gradually worse, and, as a not unnatural result,
more peevish and irritable. Madame Sand describes
him as 'a detestable patient'; she says 'he became
completely demoralised. Bearing pain courageously
enough, he could not overcome the disquietude of
his imagination. The monastery was for him full of
terrors and phantoms even when he was well.'

At last things came to such a pitch that, although he did not seem to be in a state to with-
stand the fatigue of a journey, he seemed equally
incapable of going through another week on the
island. The worst of the weather was now over, and

spring was rapidly making its appearance; therefore, taking this into consideration, Madame Sand judged it wiser to take advantage of the elements being favourable, and to leave Majorca. Her decision was no doubt in part due to the fact that, whereas Chopin had landed there with only a slight cough, he was now spitting blood, and she became seriously alarmed. They accordingly at once made arrangements for their departure for Marseilles, *vid* Barcelona. In a letter to her friend, François Rollinat, George Sand gives a terrible account of the sufferings of poor Chopin on the journey from Palma to Barcelona. After having been obliged to travel the three miles between Valdemosa and Palma, over the worst roads in the island, in a *birlocho* (a small open carriage), they embarked on a small steamboat, the only one then serving the place, which was used for the transport of pigs to Barcelona. They had for their fellow-passengers over a hundred of these animals, ' whose continual cries and foul smell left our patient neither rest nor fresh air. He arrived at Barcelona still spitting blood, and crawling along like a ghost.' However, arrived here their misfortunes were practically at an end, for the French consul, as well as the commander of one of the French war-ships at the time in harbour, both showed them very great kindness. Here they remained in the hotel for a week, Chopin being placed under the care of the ship's surgeon, who stopped the hæmorrhage from the lung in twenty-four hours. Fourteen days after leaving Palma they arrived at Marseilles, having this time been considerably more fortunate in their steamer and its captain.

Before closing this chapter it will not be out of place to select for consideration some of those compositions, other than the Preludes, which Chopin completed while staying in the Balearic Islands. Of these, the Ballade, Op. 38, and the Scherzo, Op. 39, have been discussed under their respective heads. There remains only the Opus 40, which we find to consist of two 'Polonaises.' Together with these, let us look at the remaining five Polonaises which Chopin published; Op. 26, two Polonaises; Op. 53, Polonaise in A flat; and Op. 61, Polonaise-Fantasie in A flat. First, as to the word Polonaise. The Polonaise (originally the word was spelled

'Polonais' without the final e) is a processional type of dance in ¾ time, demonstrating especially the Polish national spirit and character. The accent is generally found in the second beat of the bar, and the great rhythmical expression of the dance forms one of its greatest charms. As a form of composition it was much resorted to by Polish musicians generally, such as Prince Oginski, Elsner, Kozlowski, and others. It was a processional form of dance, in which the men rather than the women sustained the principal part, and was always the Court dance *par excellence*. Prominent amongst those composers outside of Poland who have written Polonaises are Weber and Spohr.

Of Chopin's contributions under this head, it may be said that he gradually freed himself from the conventionalities of the form in his later specimens, considerably idealising it, and colouring it with his own personality. He may be said to have almost transferred the *locale* of the dance from the ball-room to the battle-field, the Polonaises being essentially expressive of their composer's patriotic feelings, and from this point of view especially interesting.

The first of Op. 26 is in the key of C sharp minor, and is perhaps less virile than any of the others. Most beautiful is the middle *meno mosso* movement, which, to our mind, breathes 'Spohr' in nearly every bar. Notice, also, the beautiful modulatory bars 10, 11, 12, followed by the succession of sevenths, to which Chopin is so partial. But what a different spirit prevails in No. 2 of this Opus! It seems to express the subdued wrath of his politically-oppressed people. The opening semiquaver figure seems to us

most markedly expressive of this, for in itself it is essentially a figure which musical instinct would dictate should be played *forte*, yet we have *pianissimo* marked by the composer, as much as to indicate rage to which they are unable to give vent. This murmuring spirit of oppression prevails throughout the first part of the work. At the *meno mosso* the music grows calmer, until we are again led into the first theme. Notice, on the last appearance of the *sotto voce* phrase alluded to above, the numerous marks of expression—*poco rit*, the next bar *accel.*, then *rit* again, and so on, giving us a vivid picture of the unsettled and rebellious feelings at work. Especially characteristic, also, are the final bars, with their strongly marked *nuances*. No. 1 of Op. 40 is in A major, and is throughout an intensely martial composition. But there is a spirit of victory and conquest about it foreign to the last two we have just discussed. It is so well known as to render any attempt at either emotional or formal analysis unnecessary. The most remarkable circumstance attached to it seems to us to lie in the fact that it is supposed to have been written during Chopin's stay in the Carthusian monastèry. For he mentions the dedication of it to his friend Julius Fontana, in a letter written from Marseilles almost immediately after his arrival there from Palma. When we consider the conditions by which he was surrounded, the wretched health in which he was, and the thousand-and-one experiences he had to undergo, all having a tendency to depress, instead of elevate, his inspirational powers; moreover, when we compare it with the other works composed then, we find it difficult to credit that this healthy and vigorous creation had its birth at that time. We incline rather to believe that it was with this, as with some of the Preludes—that is, that it was originally composed prior to his departure from Paris, and merely completed during his stay in Majorca. The No. 2 differs from it as presenting more variety of emotion, though we must confess to finding the second portion in A flat major wanting in conciseness, and its continuous enharmonic changes somewhat irritating. The same complaint may be made with regard to the No. 1 in F sharp minor of Op. 44. It is noisy in the extreme, and with the exception of the Mazurka movement intervening, is greatly wanting in those many and varied emotional aspects which distinguish its companions. Let us select it, therefore, for more technical examination. The composer leads off with a preliminary phrase in octaves, consisting of eight bars. We are then introduced to the leading theme, which, after eight bars, is given to the bass in octaves. A full close is then made in F sharp minor, and a sudden transition hurls us into the key of B flat minor, in which we now get a short tributary to the leading theme. At the eighth and last bar of this we are, by enharmonic means, brought back to the original theme in the primary key, the effect of the transition being no less abrupt than on the occasion of our quitting it. The tributary now once more appears, slightly elaborated, and is again followed by the principal, to which is added considerable elaboration of the bass part. We are now soon to have fresh matter, notwithstanding that we see ahead of us the same and ever-recurring transitional phrase, which, at first sight, almost causes us to fear more repetition. But in this we are agreeably disappointed, for instead of B flat minor we find ourselves in A major, in which we feel much more at home. There now occurs a somewhat protracted episode, which at length gives way to an allusion in C sharp minor to the tributary of the original theme; the episode is then returned to and concluded. We now throw off the rhythm of the Polonaise for that of the Mazurka. We are still in the relative major of the primary key, and the Mazurka follows its usual course, reminding us forcibly at times of his other compositions in this form. This concluded, we are gradually led back, by allusions to the different parts of the Polonaise, to its leading theme, which is followed in much the same way as before the Mazurka movement. At the *stretto* we have the coda, conspicuous in which is a long cadenza for the left hand, which leads us into a *cantabile diminuendo*, with which the work closes. Perhaps the finest, certainly the most popular (though that is no criterion) is the Polonaise in A flat major, Op. 53, beloved of pianists one and all. The first object to attract our notice is the rushing succession of chromatic chords of the sixth, while a highly important, though perhaps not so noticeable, feature is the retention by the composer of the dominant E flat as a pedal bass on the second beat of each bar following the succession of sixths. Especially effective is this in bar 6. In bar 10 we have it again, although the effect is not so marked here, the note forming the seventh of the chord; but mark its retention in the first chord of the following bar, when it is surmounted by the E flat dominant seventh chord. Again, in the next bar, we have above it the common chord of B flat. In fact, we do not lose sight of it in this form until we find it in its place as the bass of the A flat dominant seventh, at the commencement of bar 13. Familiar, of course, to all is the realistic effect attained by the descending semiquaver figure for the left hand in octaves, which can only impress the mind with one picture,—that of the trampling of horses,—whilst in the right hand we have an intensely martial theme which augments the effect of the picture to such an extent that it does not take a very imaginative mind to grasp the whole intention of this portion of the work. This is no doubt the main reason of its enormous popularity, and if the composer ever did err on the side of realism it is here; but the end attained may fairly be said to justify the means employed. Before leaving this number we may point out the great result attained by comparatively small means in bar 17 of this part in E major. At bar 13 we find *poco a poco crescendo*. Here this especial effect may be said to begin. The climax is reached at bar 17, where the whole structure is lowered a semitone, with the effect that the entire mass of sound seems to have suddenly come upon us, whereas before it had been comparatively distant.

To follow Chopin through all the 'wanderings' of his Fantasie Polonaise, Op. 61, would take more space than we are able to command. Let it suffice that, whilst there are contained in it some of the most beautiful thoughts he has given us, yet, taken as a work of art, the whole is so terribly diffuse as to in a great measure reduce its artistic value. The constituent elements of the composition, though intensely beautiful of themselves, are not linked together as part of one organic whole. It is, perhaps, one of the most unrestrained and unsymmetrical of his compositions, for while they may often be said to consist of emotional expression quite unfettered, yet a certain coherence of form is maintained, if only by the rhythmical accent. Finally, although in these Polonaises we find some of the most remarkable and characteristic of his thoughts, they nevertheless represent only the masculine side of his genius, which does not appeal to us to such an extent as that which he has exemplified in such forms as the Ballades, Preludes, or Etudes, and although perhaps these 'feminine' forms demand greater æsthetic appreciation on the part of the listener, yet they seem to us more reflective of the composer himself, and therefore the most satisfying.

CHAPTER XI

In the last chapter we left Madame Sand and her party safely landed in Marseilles. Here they were sufficiently fortunate to secure the services of a physician in every way capable of treating the invalid, and to this reason may be attributed the somewhat lengthy stay made by them in that town. Under the care of Dr. Cauvière (the physician named by George Sand in her letters from Marseilles) Chopin's health rapidly improved. From this time forward we find a much brighter tone prevailing in his letters to his various friends. To Fontana he writes:—'My health is still improving. I begin to eat, walk, and speak like other men; and when you receive these few words from me you will see that I again write with ease.' He busied himself with negotiating with publishers for the sale of several MSS. (mostly those written at Palma), and altogether seemed to emerge from the lethargic state into which he had lapsed during the latter part of his sojourn at Valdemosa.

Both musician and novelist were equally glad to have turned their backs upon the place in which their stay had been fraught with so much misery, although the city of Marseilles itself did not hold out any inducements likely to retain either for a longer time than was strictly necessary. In another letter, written to Fontana at this time, we find mention of his being so far recovered as to have been able to assist at the funeral service of the famous opera tenor, Adolphe Nourrit, who had, in a fit of despondency, committed suicide by throwing himself from a window in Naples. His body was taken by his widow to Paris *viâ* Marseilles, at which latter place a funeral service was held in the Church of Notre-Dame-du-Mont. It was at this service that Chopin lent his assistance by playing the organ at the Elevation. The audience, some of whom had paid as much as fifty centimes each for a seat (an unusually high price), seem to have been keenly disappointed at the value received in return for their reckless expenditure, expecting, no doubt, in place of the refined playing of the performer, that he would give them noise no less great than what they naturally expected from a man with such a great reputation.   Apart from his artistic feelings in the matter, poor Chopin was no doubt fearful of the result should he tax the resources of the wretched instrument to any great extent, for, says Madame Sand, 'What an organ!   A false, screaming instrument, which had no wind, except for the purpose of being out of tune. . . . He, however, made the most of it, taking the least shrill stops, and playing *Les Astres*,[1] not in the enthusiastic manner in which Nourrit used to sing it, but plaintively and softly, like the far-off echo from another world.'

From Marseilles they made a short tour in Italy, visiting Genoa and the neighbourhood, after which they returned once more *viâ* Marseilles to Nohant, a hamlet lying some three miles from the little town of La Châtre, in the department of Indre.   Here Madame Sand had her home, and here it was that Chopin passed some three or four months of nearly

---

[1] A melody of Schubert's.

every year from 1838 to 1846. The Château of Nohant, as it was called, was a plain grey stone house, the principal feature of which was its steep Mansarde roofs of the time of Louis XVI.,—a picturesque house, standing back from the road, and surrounded by a large flower garden and spinney, and having quite the air of repose of an English manor-house. Arrived here, Chopin, who now seemed to be on the sure road to recovery, was attended by a physician and old friend of Madame Sand's, Dr. Papet, who expressed himself confident that any signs of serious pulmonary affection that had formerly showed themselves had entirely vanished, and that there need not be the slightest cause for alarm. The quiet country life passed at Nohant, although undoubtedly beneficial to him physically, did not suit Chopin. He chafed under the monotony of 'every day's most quiet need,' and longed for his Paris; but with Madame Sand it was just the reverse; in fact, she often contemplated settling down entirely at Nohant, for she says:—'Parisian life strains our nerves and kills us in the end. Ah! how I hate it, that centre of light. I would never set foot in it again if only the people

I like would make the same resolution. At Paris I am always ill, both in body and soul.'

Chopin's letters at this time consist mostly of instructions to his friend Fontana in Paris, with respect to the sale of his manuscripts. He seems to have taken for his motto (in some cases, no doubt, with good cause), ' Barabbas was a publisher.' Certainly, on many occasions the sums received for the sale of his copyrights seem utterly inadequate, even when one takes into consideration the comparatively small sale then attained by his works. Nevertheless, midst all this wrangling and complaining, there frequently shows itself that vein of humour and sarcasm which formed no small part of Chopin's character. For instance, he commences, in one letter to Fontana, ' The best part of your letter is your address, which I had already forgotten, and without which I do not know if I would have answered you so soon.' And in a later letter to the same friend, amongst other commissions given, he says :—' Find me a valet, and kiss Madame Leo [1] (surely the first commission will be the more

<hr>

[1] Wife of August Leo, his banker.

pleasant to you, wherefore I relieve you of the second
if you will do the first).   Tell Gutmann that I was
much pleased that he asked for me at least once.
To Moscheles, should he be in Paris, order to be given
an infusion of Neukomm's Oratorios prepared with
Berlioz's Cellini and Doehler's Concerto.   You yourself take a bath in whale's infusion as a restorative
from all the commissions I give you, which I know
you will willingly do for me to the greatest extent
in your power.   I will do the same for you when
you are married; only not to Ox, for that is my
party.'   In such like banter he frequently indulges;
indeed, when we consider the state of his health his
light-heartedness is at times amazing.   But he was
quite a creature of impulse, now as gay and bright
as a boy, and the next half hour would find him
plunged in the deepest dejection.   A spirit of
intense restlessness would sometimes come over him;
as Madame Sand says, ' Chopin was always wishing
for Nohant, yet he never could bear it.'   He was
no sooner in the country than he longed for the
gaiety and life of the town.   Yet life at Nohant
was not by any means confined to work, and such

simple and rural pleasures as one generally looks for and gets in the country. On the contrary, Madame Sand seems to have left nothing undone to make the time go by. Billiards, shooting, fishing, boating, and such like sports were freely indulged in by the novelist and her guests; amongst whom were frequently to be found such names as Pauline Garcia, Eugène Delacroix, and the Comtesse d'Agoult. Private theatricals was a frequent form of amusement, and Eugène Delacroix, the artist, in one of his letters mentions a grand ball given by Madame Sand to the peasants of the neighbourhood. Nevertheless, the monotony of the life became intensely wearisome to Chopin. Thus it is that we have him writing urgent and imperative requests to his friend Fontana to find him suitable apartments, and to expect his speedy return; and not only for Chopin did the good Fontana busy himself, but for Madame Sand who, when she found Chopin determined to leave, would not let him out of her sight, and followed him to Paris.

Fontana was certainly nothing less than an angel in human form if he carried out one-half of the commissions entrusted to him. For Chopin's letters simply teem with trifling requests to his friend. Of the management of the more prosaic details of life he was quite incapable, and readily threw the burden of it upon his friends; although this manner of trespassing upon their good nature did not—as in the case of Richard Wagner, for instance—take the form of repeated requests for money. On the contrary, Chopin, although decidedly an extravagant man, liking and ordering the best of everything, was generally in a position to support his tastes by his own exertions. He was scrupulously tidy and clean, and most particular in his dress. He evidently did not think it incumbent upon genius to simulate the attire of a second-hand clothes dealer, or the manners of a coal-heaver,—far from it; he was essentially a gentleman in every sense of the word, and no doubt this it was that, coupled with his undeniable genius, made Frederic Chopin one of the most striking and original men of his time. For how seldom do we ever find the two together, or for that matter even separately.

At length the long-suffering Fontana succeeded in

finding suitable rooms for both Chopin and Madame Sand; for the former in the Rue Tronchet, and for the latter in the Rue Pigalle; but this done, there remained the thousand-and-one little items about which Chopin was so faddy. For instance, after writing some pages descriptive of the smallest details, such as, 'The rooms must, of course, have inlaid floors, newly laid if possible, and require no repairs. . . There must be perfect quietness, and no blacksmith in the neighbourhood; further, there must be no smoke nor bad smells, but a fine view and large garden. Find something splendid.' And again, 'In the ante-room you will hang the grey curtains which were in my cabinet with the piano, and in the bedroom the same as before, only under them the white muslin, over which before were under the grey ones. If the little sofa, that which stood in the dining-room, could be covered with red, in the same stuff with which the chairs are covered, it might then be placed in the drawing-room.' Then he would leave the subject of the rooms and furniture for a time, and give instructions about his wardrobe in this wise:—'Go to my tailors, Dauilemont's, on the Boulevards, and order him to make me at once a pair of grey trousers, something respectable, not striped, but plain and elastic; you know what I require.   Also a quiet black velvet waistcoat, with very little and no loud pattern,—something very quiet but very elegant. Write constantly to me—three times a day if you like, whether you have anything to say or not.'   And after all this and a hundred other things he would finally end by adding, 'Now, for God's sake, I beg of you take an *active* [the italics are ours] interest in the matter!'   It is difficult to find words sufficiently strong to convey any idea of the 'activity' which his friend must have displayed, did he faithfully carry out one-half of the things entrusted to him.   That he proved worthy of his trust we may see from the fact that, in October 1839, we find Chopin duly installed in the Rue Tronchet, and Madame Sand in the Rue Pigalle.   Once settled down, Chopin resumed his teaching, and generally took up the threads of his former Parisian life where he had laid them down on his departure.

He now made the acquaintance of Moscheles, whose

remarks on the artist's playing and compositions are perhaps worthy of note. Moscheles found his *ad libitum* playing, as he called it, full of charm, and he goes on to say, 'The dilettantish harsh modulations which strike me disagreeably, when I am playing his compositions, no longer shock me, because he glides lightly over them in a fairy-like way with his delicate fingers. His *piano* is so softly breathed forth that he does not require any strong *forte* to produce the wished-for contrasts.'

It was with Moscheles that Chopin played at this time at the Court of Louis Philippe at St. Cloud; the chief work performed being the former musician's Sonata in E flat major, for four hands. One result of this visit was a presentation by the king to Chopin of a gold cup and saucer, while to Moscheles was presented a travelling case, which Chopin caustically told him was given with the object of getting the sooner rid of him. During this year the Preludes only were published, but the time spent at Nohant had been fruitful, for these were followed by several other works, amongst which we may mention the Sonata in B flat minor, Op. 35, containing the now celebrated funeral march, which had, however, been written prior to the accompanying movement. In addition to these were, Impromptu, F sharp major, Op. 36; the second Ballade, Op. 38; the third Scherzo, Op. 39; Two Polonaises, Op. 40; Four Mazurkas, Op. 41; Valse in A flat major, Op. 42; Tarantella, Allegro de Concert, and Fantaisie, Op. 49. We will now proceed to notice the Sonata, Op. 35, taking with it its companions, Op. 58, and the Op. 65, for violoncello and pianoforte, which, with the early Op. 4, comprise the master's contributions in this form.

The B flat minor Sonata commences with a preamble of four bars, *grave,* after which the leading theme in a *doppio movimento* is announced. This becomes more and more agitated as it develops, until the second subject in the key of D flat major is reached. This second subject is, we think, the best in the first movement. Later we get this theme varied, and with a florid bass, and followed by an episode in triplets (crotchet). With the short working out of this episode the first portion of the opening movement closes. We are, after the repeat, led off with an episode, built more or less upon the leading motive. The working out of this is extremely tantalising, for we are led through so many different keys, and there is so little that is straightforward, that by the time relief (in the shape of the counter theme, now in B flat major) arrives we are almost too bewildered to appreciate it. The coda is a short one, consisting only of some twelve bars. The leading theme of the Scherzo commences in E flat minor, and ends in F sharp minor, and is followed by a continuation on the theme, of which chromatic successions of chords of the sixth are a prominent feature. At the *più lento* we have a trio in G flat major, which after some sixty-four bars comes to a full close on the tonic. After a short continuation of this the first section of the Scherzo is repeated.

Of the *Marche Funèbre* we need not speak further than to say that it is by far the most consistent and beautiful movement of the Sonata. As to the state of mind in which the composer was when he wrote the final *presto*, we do not hazard an opinion. It is most curious music, and musically speaking has not the remotest connection, thematic or otherwise, with anything in the Sonata. With regard to this finale, which is a kind of unharmonised *toccata*, Chopin

P

stated in one of his letters to Fontana that the left hand *unisono* with the right hand was supposed to be gossiping after the march, which Mr. Niecks says he takes to mean that 'after the burial the good neighbours took to discussing the merits of the departed, not without a spice of backbiting.' Perhaps so; but if such were the case, the 'backbiting' is certainly more forcibly expressed in the music than is the 'discussion of merits,' which fact augurs badly either for the mourners or the deceased.

The second Sonata in B minor was not published until some five years later. It is certainly the most interesting of all, and there is a wealth of material and a lavishness in its use which distinctly shows what a store its composer possessed. All the melodies are in themselves beautiful, but they are also entirely independent, and have no affinity with one another. The musical matter of which the opening bars of the first movement consist is very diffuse. Forcibly marked rhythms and rushing chromatic passages prevail until we reach the melody in D major, which forms the second subject, if indeed we can be said to have already had a first subject proper. As the work proceeds it becomes more intelligible, and the melody is supremely lovely, while the elaboration and general handling of the subsidiary portion of the second subject is replete with finesse and harmonic cunning. The Scherzo itself is delightful; the contrast attained by the *sostenuto* portion in B major, coming after the delicate quaver figures of the first section, is highly effective. In the third movement the composer wanders considerably, with the result that the effect attained is that of an improvisation rather than of a definitely designed portion of a whole. The introductory bars of the finale are almost cacophonous; and after the eighth bar we are launched once more upon a sea of trouble in the form of an *agitato* movement ($\frac{9}{8}$); which after a while gives way to some delicate descending scale passages in semiquavers, followed each time by a plaintive quaver phrase, which breathes nothing but sorrow. Notice further on the variety of effect obtained by the change from the two beats of three quavers to the two beats of four quavers each, in the accompaniment of the first subject, which continues until we again reach the descending semiquavers with the querulous bars intervening. The right hand is now entirely occupied with the undulating semi-quaver passages untill we finally come upon the initial theme, which, after it has been repeated in octaves, leads us into the key of B major, in which the work closes.

The last and perhaps the most unsatisfactory of the Sonatas is the Op. 65, in G minor, for violoncello and piano. On reading this composition we can only pause and wonder why the musician expended so much labour and time on work which must have been uncongenial to him, and for which he was in no way fitted. A pure romanticist was Frederic Chopin, and as a consequence his best music is his programme-music : that is, music in which the 'programme' is an emotional schedule expressive of the ideas and feelings within the composer when he wrote. Could anything be more antagonistic to the classic form of the sonata? Consequently we find him here, as in the Concertos, continually endeavouring to repress the ideas within him which were clamouring for utterance, as unsuitable to the form in which he was writing. The music given to us by Beethoven in his pianoforte sonatas is 'abstract music,' whereas undoubtedly the *real* meaning of such of Chopin's works as the Ballades, Polonaises, Preludes, or Scherzos is reserved for him who can find the key to their emotional basis. That this 'programme-music' is superior to abstract music we do not for one moment imply, for it is a subject for much discussion; but that it was the means by which Chopin best expressed himself is patent to all who have given themselves diligently to the study of his work. It is sufficiently manifest that Chopin's nature rendered him incapable of the creation of music wholly for its own sake. It of necessity must take the colour of his emotions at the time it was written. Therefore it is obvious that it is in some measure to his life we must look before we can arrive at the full understanding of the composer's meaning. Yet it must not be thought that Chopin wished his music to be valued for the arbitrary meaning attached to it. Had he written it with this idea, we venture to say the result would have been to him disastrous. It was merely the nature of the man to reflect in his music his life, and the thoughts which had their creation in the episodes of that life. He was no Wagner. He was no Berlioz. Had he, as we have said, expected his hearers to trace the source of his inspiration and to gather one and the same meaning from any one composition, he would have dismally failed in his object; for, no matter how poetically suggestive music may be to the man who created it, it will in all probability convey a hundred different impressions to as many listeners, each impression being of necessity coloured by the individuality of its recipient. What we mean is that Chopin used his poetic-basis more as a *means* than an *end*. He expressed his thoughts as he wrote, and subordinated them to nothing; whereas the composer who writes 'absolute' music, such as is in its place in the sonata, is he whose melodic, harmonic, and rhythmical senses once stirred, can evolve sounds beautiful and interesting in themselves, from out which again arise developments almost endless in proportion to the musical instinct, invention, and command of technique of the composer; and the whole of which he subordinates to the form in which he is writing. That he have an imagination is of course as essential in the one case as in the other; but the fact remains that what is art with the one is not so for the other, for it has not the same aims, nor does it rest upon the same foundation. And when we have regard to this, can we wonder at or question the truth of (at all events as regards the Sonatas) Liszt's judgment when he said that they contained '*plus de volonté que d'inspiration*'?

CHAPTER XII

WE have now reached the time which saw Chopin's
power not only as a composer, but as a pianist, at
its zenith. And although he is known to have de-
tested playing in public, he, nevertheless, recognised
the necessity of occasionally playing at a concert as
a concomitant of his position. Thus, in April 1841,
we find him giving a concert at Pleyel's rooms. The
audience seems to have been a semi-private one, consisting, for the most part, of his intimate friends,
pupils, and pupils' friends; whilst amongst the
artists we find the names of Madame Damoreau-
Cinti, an operatic artist of the first water, and
Heinrich Ernst, the violinist. Liszt describes the
audience in this ¦wise:—'Last Monday, at eight
o'clock in the evening, Mr. Pleyel's rooms were
brilliantly lit up; numerous carriages kept bringing

to the foot of the staircase, covered with carpet and
perfumed with flowers, the most elegant women, the
most fashionable men, the most celebrated artists,
the wealthiest financiers; in fact, a whole *élite* of
society,—a whole aristocracy of birth, fortune, talent,
and beauty.' Chopin, taking advantage of his refined
audience, selected for performance at this concert his
more ideal and *spirituel* works, such as the Preludes,
Studies, Nocturnes, and Mazurkas; and seems to
have had his audience *en rapport* with him throughout the concert. Liszt tells us that two of the
Etudes and a Ballade were encored, and that, had
it not been out of consideration for Chopin, who
seemed so weak and fatigued, they would not have
rested content until every item had been repeated.
However, it is gratifying to know that the success
of the concert was sufficient to encourage Chopin to
repeat it within the twelve months. This second
concert took place in the following February, and
amongst the artists on this occasion we find the
names of Madame Viardot Garcia and Franchomme,
the 'cellist. It was in every way as successful as its
predecessor, Chopin entirely charming his audience

with his renderings of such of his works as the
Ballade in A flat, Prelude in D flat, four Nocturnes,
and three of his Mazurkas. One and all were
astonished at the marvellous effects produced by
Chopin from his piano. The delicacy of his touch,
the nimbleness of his fingers, and the perfect and
minute technique, added to the personality infused
into all he did, gained for him the highest rank as
a pianist.

From amid the many distinctive features of
Chopin's pianoforte 'style,' two shine out very prominently. They are the employment of the *tempo
rubato*, and the revolution in the use of the pedals.
From the literal meaning of *tempo rubato*, which is
'robbed time,' we do not get the full significance of
the expression. Indeed, it has been the receptacle
of severally different interpretations, according to the
ideas of the several composers who have used it.
And we find that Chopin's intention when employing
it differs considerably from that of other musicians.
But the meaning of the phrase as he uses it is indicated pretty clearly in his method of writing, for
no matter how freely he may write for one hand,

the other is invariably employed to mark the regular beat and rhythm. Many critics, in speaking of Chopin's playing, have taken particular exception to this 'exaggerated phrasing,' but Chopin never intended that the rhythm should be in any way obscured by indulgence in the *tempo rubato.* He no doubt originally conceived the idea from the recitatives of the Italian composers of his time. For instance, glance for one moment at the recitative music introduced in the Larghetto movement of the F minor Concerto, and also at the *Etude* in C sharp minor of Op. 25, which commences with the following phrase of recitative :—

The requisite interpretation of this phrase could not be given by any other instrument than the piano, and it is perhaps one of the best examples of purely instrumental music as a means of unfettered emotional expression. Yet it would, if played in any strict time, entirely lose the reason for its existence. Consequently, its right interpretation must be left, if not entirely, to a very large extent to the instinct of the player.

Liszt has given us quite a true reflection of his own nature in the construction which he put upon the phrase *tempo rubato*. He says: 'Suppose a tree bent by the wind, the wind stirs up life amongst the leaves, whilst between them pass the rays of the sun, and a trembling light is the result: this is what Chopin means by the *rubato*.' This is just what one would have expected from Liszt, very fanciful and akin to poetical; but it brings us no nearer to the gist of the thing. In points like these it is that we specially feel the loss of the 'pianoforte-method' which Chopin engaged himself upon in the latter years of his life, but which was, unfortunately, together with many letters and other valuable relics, burnt. It is difficult, nay, impossible, to find a word which will convey fully Chopin's meaning in this respect. Dr. Hanslick has referred to it as 'a morbid unsteadiness of *tempo*,' which is unnecessarily severe. It undoubtedly means much more than the mere 'robbing' of one note and giving to the next, and it is with a genius of the *genre* of that of Chopin that we specially feel the inadequacy of the present system of musical signs to fully convey to us the full beauty of his conceptions. As Liszt may be said to have developed the powers of touch, so may Chopin be said to have fully revealed the possibilities of the pedal as an adjunct to pianoforte playing. Pianoforte pedals made their first appearance in this country towards the latter end of the last century, when they were introduced by the famous makers, Messrs. Broadwood. It was reserved for Chopin and Liszt to demonstrate their true value. Hitherto they had been only used by pianists to obtain contrasts of *piano* and *forte*, and to Chopin especially is due the revelation of their use as a means for the production of an ever-varying tone colour. For instance, the extended harmonies so freely indulged in by Chopin lose half their beauty when deprived of the assistance of the pedal; for, if judiciously used, we are able by its aid to increase the richness and beauty of the chord, allowing the harmonies to vibrate with the fundamental tone. Again, for the purpose of gaining an exceptionally *legato* effect,

Chopin frequently used the pedal, immediately after striking the chord, in this manner :—

Here we have indicated the pressing down of the pedal by the quaver note and the raising of the same by the quaver rest, on the line below. We are, of course, alluding now to the right, or what is commonly called 'loud' pedal. Specially noticeable, also, is the use made by Chopin of the 'soft' pedal, and the combination of both pedals. By their aid he gave an indefinite charm to many passages, particularly to those enharmonic modulations to which he was so partial. In such cases he would attain a kind of 'veiled' effect, considerably idealising passages which, in the hands of some performers, might have sounded unsympathetic, if not harsh. Thus it was that his favourite piano was a Pleyel, mainly on account of their touch and pedal action, which, Liszt says, 'enabled him to draw from them sounds which one might have believed to belong to those harmonicas of which Germany has retained the monopoly.' How he would have revelled, had he lived to-day, in the pianofortes of Blüthner or Steinway!

Amongst the pupils of Chopin at this time we find such well-known English names as Brinley Richards and Lindsay Sloper. He also had several transactions relating to the publication here of his works with Messrs. Wessel (now Messrs. Ashdown) and Cramer and Beale and Co.; whilst amongst his publishers for France and Germany respectively were MM. Schlesinger and Co., Troupenas and Cie, Pleyel, Richault, Breitkopf and Härtel (to whose edition of his complete works we have gone for this work), Schott's Söhne, Schuberth and Co., and Gebethner and Wolff of Warsaw. The first appearance of his work published in England was in or about the year 1836. He always endeavoured to publish such works as he from time to time brought out simultaneously in the three countries; but reference to the dates of their several appearances shows that he was seldom enabled to do so. The years 1842-47 were highly prolific, for during that time there appeared all the works whose Opus numbers range from 51 to 65. These include many of the Nocturnes, Mazurkas, Valses, besides the Berceuse in D flat major. During these years he divided his time between Paris and Nohant, with the exception of 1840. As to his whereabouts at that time we have no authentic facts; but as Madame Sand did not go to Nohant, it may be pretty safely assumed that he remained in Paris. During this time there is no doubt that Madame

Sand was most assiduous in her attention to and thought for Chopin, and no matter in what light we may view her later actions towards him we can, but in justice, give her the credit of her devotion to the artist. And although we are not in the least inclined to view her later attitude in any lenient light, yet we cannot fail to see that her sex, her anomalous position and freedom of expression and action did not in any degree tend to soften the tongues of those whose animosity she provoked. Inasmuch as she kept his accounts, wrote many of his letters, and tended him with the greatest of devotion in the many trying times when the disease laid him up, she is worthy of some praise. Moreover, her care for his physical wants was only a part of the benefits which he derived from her friendship. In her house he passed many happy hours; he would frequently drop in and play or talk as he felt inclined, and was sure of being undisturbed. Then, again, the quiet country life which he passed at Nohant was, although frequently uncongenial to him, highly beneficial in his state of health. Apart from society acquaintances, the only other friends at whose house he cared to visit to any extent were Madame Leo and her husband. And yet we find Chopin speaking of this couple in his letters in 'a manner which savours of nothing so much as ingratitude. No doubt they sometimes formed a source of irritation to his highly strung disposition; but even granting this, when we consider the kindness shown him by the banker and his wife, we cannot but come to the conclusion that he frequently showed himself quite insensible to the many kindnesses he received. Nor was it only with respect to Madame Leo and her husband that he was remiss. We have seen of what invaluable service Fontana was to Chopin, and the enormous amount of personal trouble to which he put himself on his friend's behalf. Yet we very rarely find in his later letters any expression of gratitude, nor do we find the composer returning these obligations in the many small ways in which he could have done so, beyond the fact of on one occasion dedicating two of his Polonaises, Op. 40, to Fontana. And this caused him no personal effort. He was not the man to put himself out in any way for his

friends.   Therefore, when we weigh all these things
in the balance, we cannot but think that, albeit
what fault there was in their connection lay on the
shoulders of the novelist, yet she on her side had
some reasonable ground for complaint.

Let us for one moment consider some of the things
which Madame Sand says of him in her *Histoire*.
She complains that 'He accepted nothing in reality.
This was his vice and his virtue, his grandeur and his
misery.   Implacable to the least blemish he had an
immense enthusiasm for the least light; his imagination frequently seeing in it a sun.'   Again, she says :
' At no time was the friendship of Chopin for me a
refuge in sadness.'   Moreover, we know that Chopin
latterly showed a great aversion to the children of
Madame Sand.   That these defects in Chopin's
character did not have their creation in the brain
of the novelist is in some degree proved by their sub-
stantiation by Liszt.   If we set ourselves to find
excuse for them, we might throw the burden upon
his nationality, for the Poles are essentially a nation
with whom a sense of individual importance and
gratification is not the least noticeable characteristic.

Such, however, is not our intention, although we admit that if this were innate, it was probably more prominently developed in the later years of his life by the state of his health.

But to pass once more from the man to his work. The principal groups of pianoforte composition now remaining for discussion are the Impromptus and Waltzes. Of the first named we have four. Three were published during the composer's lifetime, while the fourth is a posthumous publication. Their Opus numbers are Op. 29, 36, 51, and 66. The Op. 29 in A flat is one of the most spontaneous and beautiful of any of his works. Especially so is the opening phrase. In the first two bars one is struck by the peculiar whirring effect obtained by the use of the D natural against the dominant E flat in the left hand.

Wagner has used the same means for his 'Spinning Wheel Chorus' in the *Flying Dutchman* (we quote from Liszt's pianoforte transcription).

On reaching the *sostenuto* in F minor, we have a great contrast; the movement here becoming more akin to the Nocturne. Notice at the closing bars of this section, just before the re-entry of the initial phrase, the effects gained by the composer by the use of the dominant harmony of F, leading the ear to expect the tonic, instead of which the dominant seventh chord is left unresolved, and after this bar we are led straight into the first subject in A flat, in this wise.

The effect is deliciously surprising, and certainly in

its place in an Impromptu. The first movement of the second Impromptu in F sharp major is also in the Nocturne style, and tonic and dominant harmony prevail for the most part. Especially beautiful is the phrase commencing at bar 30, and continuing until we reach the movement in D natural. This reminds us somewhat in style of the middle section of the Polonaise in A flat, Op. 53. The theme assumes an exceptionally bold character when accompanied a few bars later by the bass figure in octaves. Perhaps exception might be taken by purists to the last two bars of this part leading into the key of F major. We now have the original theme slightly modified with an accompaniment of quaver triplets. The composer then indulges in elaborate ornamentation for the right hand, while the left hand plays a melodious inner and bass part. The Impromptu closes with the phrase alluded to at bar 30. Its whole tone is softer, and more cogitative than that of the preceding one, while in parts it certainly seems to be descriptive of definite events in the mind of the composer when he wrote it.

No. 3 opens brightly, and is more similar in its

' manner' to the first in A flat. In this first movement we again find the composer more or less in his
Nocturne style, while the *sostenuto* involuntarily
calls up recollections of the Etude in C sharp minor.
It is by no means the best of the group. This brings
us to the end of the Impromptus proper.

The fourth, commonly called Fantasia-Impromptu,
was, as we have before noted, published after the
composer's death by his friend Fontana. It is one of
the most delightful of his conceptions. The opening
allegro agitato, with its rushing semiquaver figure
and quaver triplet accompaniment, breathes spontaneity in every bar, while the *largo* portion in D
flat contains some of the master's choicest thoughts.
It is so well known, and such a favourite in our
concert halls, as to need no detailed description.
But we cannot refrain from noticing the closing
phrase of eight bars where the melody—previously
given at the *largo* in D flat—rhythmically and melodically modified is taken up in the left hand, while
the right hand accompanies with the semiquaver
figures *pianissimo*. It is one of the most beautiful
effects to be found in his works.

Before proceeding to notice the Waltzes, we propose glancing for a moment at some of the miscellaneous compositions named in the last chapter, such as the Tarantella, Op. 43; the Allegro de Concert, Op. 46; and the Fantaisie, Op. 49. Of the form in which Stephen Heller so excelled the Op. 43 is the only sample which we have from Chopin, and that we have this is no doubt due to his admiration for Rossini's Tarantella (*soirées musicales*). He frequently refers to this composition in his letters, and the details of its publication seem to have caused him more annoyance than any of the other works. To agree *in toto* with Schumann's verdict of this composition would be not to give the work its due, for, says Schumann, ' Nobody can call that music.' Nevertheless, it cannot be said to be wholly successful. The tarantella is one of the very few dances which are of real Italian origin, and receives its name from the province of Taranto, its native part. But in this Tarantella of Chopin's we have more of Spanish colour than Italian. Especially is this the case in the middle portion of the work, which is perhaps the best. It is certainly more Spanish in tone than the Bolero, Op. 19. But in connection with the Allegro, Op. 46, we are certainly disposed to accept the statement of Schumann as correct. He declared that it was originally written for pianoforte and orchestra. Certain it is that no one could play the first portion of the work and not be struck by the *genre* of the music. It is undoubtedly the same as that which stands for orchestral music in the Concertos; but in the second portion of the piece this is not so, the elaborate passage work being eminently that of the piano. The work, as a whole, does not possess any great poetic beauty. But what a contrast we find in the Fantaisie, Op. 49. The very title predicts to him who knows Chopin what he may expect, as much as does the Sonata in the opposite direction. Here we find the composer glorying in his emancipation. We open with a bold phrase of two bars in octaves. This, with its responsive phrase, forms the matter for the first twenty bars. Nevertheless, we cannot refrain from pointing out the very unsatisfactory effect of the transition contained in the last two bars here;—the nineteenth and twentieth from the commencement.

But such things as these are a thousand times atoned for by what follows. Especially would we draw attention to the syncopated *agitato* melody commencing at bar 67, and the even more beautiful portion commencing some ten bars later in A flat. This is one of the most spontaneous passages in the work. Some twenty-four bars after quitting this theme we come to a very effective pianoforte passage of octaves in contrary motion, and very similar to those in the third Ballade (*vide* bars 26 and following few bars). Notice some twelve bars later the even march-like music, with its firmly moving bass and plain-chord progessions. Later on we have a repetition of the phrase in A flat, to which we alluded, this time in the key of G flat. There is now nothing to call for particular notice until we reach the *lento sostenuto*, where we get a change in both time and key. This section in B major continues now for twenty-four bars, and the musical matter which follows presents nothing striking until we come to the *adagio recitative*. With this the work practically closes, the musical matter which follows consisting only of some twelve bars of ascending quaver triplets. Amongst all these works in the somewhat larger forms essayed by Chopin we are inclined to give this a prominent place, for the composer never seems to lose grip of his subject, as is so frequently the case in the other works of the same class. The whole handling of the material is more masterly, and we do not experience that feeling of unrest to nearly so great an extent in this Fantasia, while the material itself is, as is ever the case with Chopin, original and beautiful.

CHAPTER XIII

WE now come to one of the most eventful years of Chopin's life—1847. Exactly ten years previously he had made the acquaintance of which this year was to see the severance. Had he been spared to us for another twenty years, it would have been difficult to say which event was the more important of the two, either to him or to us. But with the latter event only have we now to deal. As the accounts of this bitter ending of so much affection differ so vastly, and are so biassed either in favour of one or the other of the parties, we can only consider the statements of facts which are beyond doubt, and form our own view of the case, from what we have already seen of the lives and characters of those concerned. Perhaps it may be best to consider the lady's statement first. In her *Histoire*, Madame Sand puts forward as the reason for her action Chopin's dislike of, and disagreement with, her children, and that on her intervention on their behalf, a quarrel ensued, upon which they parted. This, so far as we know, is the only plea advanced by the novelist. From this, the assertions of such a friend of the principals as Franchomme, the 'cellist, differ widely. Mr. Frederick Niecks tells us that he obtained from him the assurance, both by letter and word of mouth, that the rupture between Chopin and Madame Sand came about in this way:—'In June 1847 Chopin was making ready to start for Nohant, when he received a letter from Madame Sand to the effect that she had just turned out her daughter and son-in-law, and that if he [Chopin] received them in his house, all would be over between them. I was with Chopin at the time the letter arrived, and he said to me, "They have only me; should I close my door upon them? No, I shall not do it!" and he did not do it, and yet he knew that this creature whom he adored would not forgive him for it. Poor friend, how I have seen him suffer!'

Surely the one explanation is as unsatisfactory as the other. It seems incredible, and indeed to us impossible, to believe that either of these trivial circumstances should have been a reason sufficient in itself to bring about a separation between these two, who had for ten long years been inseparable. And we may pretty confidently assume that such was not the case. Madame Sand had at this time just married her daughter Solange, to Clesinger the sculptor, with whom, according to the evidence of her letters, she appears to have been much pleased, and to have highly approved of the match. And it is equally difficult to believe that she turned the daughter and her husband out of her house, under the circumstances which Franchomme gives as her reason. Here is the story referred to :—

It appears that Madame Clesinger had not been treated with what her husband deemed her due in the matter of courtesy by a gentleman staying in the house at Nohant, the slight singled out for exception being that, one morning, the gentleman passed Madame Clesinger without removing his hat. On his remissness Clesinger demanded that he should straightway apologise and salute Madame Clesinger. On his refusal to do so, Clesinger is stated to have struck him, and Madame Sand being a witness of the whole proceeding, rushed downstairs and forthwith boxed the ears of the irate Clesinger, and turned him and his wife out of the house. Were we dealing with children, and the nursery our scene, we might accept this story. But when we think that the parties concerned were men and women of the world, it is laughable, and to accept it seriously, as sufficient reason for Madame Sand's action towards her own daughter, impossible. On looking carefully into both cases, we can only come to one conclusion, and that is, that, as regards her separation from Chopin, she was only waiting some suitable opportunity to bring into effect what she was inwardly wishing and longing for. There is no doubt she was weary of him, tired of nursing him, and of his increasing irritability, and seeing that this was so, either of the reasons alleged for the separation above would have been equally suitable. Therefore it matters little to us which of them she chose as a means of bringing to pass what she wished. It has also been stated, on good authority, that Madame Sand was jealous of her daughter's frequent visits to Chopin, and even if such were the case, it is certainly no more a feasible reason for her

action, both in turning out her daughter and forbidding
Chopin to receive her, than the trivial story related
by Franchomme. But be that as it may, in 1847
Chopin abruptly parted with George Sand, and never
spoke to her again. In March of the next year they
met at the house of a mutual friend, but although
Madame Sand made an advance to speak to the man
she had cast off, he did not respond, and passed her by
in silence. About this time there appeared a novel
from the pen of George Sand, entitled *Lucrezia
Floriani*. In this work the novelist has been accused
of representing Chopin to the world in the guise of
one of its principal characters, that of Prince Karol;
in fact, the charge brought against her has in some
cases been that the character was written with
premeditated intent to bring about a quarrel between
Chopin and herself. Chopin's Polish biographer,
Karasowski, further asserts that 'out of refined
cruelty, the proof-sheets were handed to Chopin with
the request to correct the misprints,' and goes on to
relate how the children of the novelist taunted the
musician by saying to him: 'M. Chopin, do you know
that Prince Karol is meant for you?' Against all

these accusations Madame Sand tries hard to defend herself. She says:—'I have drawn in Prince Karol the character of a man determined in his nature, exclusive in his sentiments, exclusive in his exigencies. Chopin was not such. Nature does not like art, design, no matter how realistic it may be. Moreover, Prince Karol is not an artist. He is a dreamer and nothing more; having no genius, he has not the rights of genius. He is, therefore, a character more true than amiable, and the portrait is so little that of a great artist such as Chopin, that he himself on reading the manuscript had not the slightest inclination to deceive himself, he, who was in other matters so suspicious.'

She goes on to say that it was only on the pointing out to him by friends, or rather enemies, that he concluded that in the character was intended a portrait of himself. But her arguments cannot be said, to use a colloquialism, 'to hold water.' It seems to us that, despite the imagination with which the novelist has surrounded the character, there is quite sufficient of reality to enable anyone to identify Prince Karol with Frederic Chopin. That the character was drawn and moulded by her intimate knowledge of

Chopin's seems certain. But to say that, in the first
instance, it was written with the deliberate intent of
exposing his weaknesses, and thus causing him pain
would perhaps be unjust without further proof than
that which exists; nevertheless, it is much to be
regretted that Madame Sand's good taste did not
prove strong enough to prevent her choosing her
most intimate companion as the subject upon which
to exercise, either for the benefit of art or the
public, her powers of analysis and imagination. The
result of all this was the immediate aggravation of
his disease. He felt his treatment by this woman
acutely. This it was in great measure, coupled with
the political disturbances which now took place in
Paris, that decided him to put into execution his
long-planned project of again visiting England.

Before, however, we follow his life in this
country, we must not omit to notice the concert
given by Chopin in Paris previous to his departure.
This took place in February 1848, at Pleyel's Rooms,
and was in some respects the most important of all
the concerts given by him. The programme included
such of his works as the *Barcarolle* and *Berceuse*,

and several of the smaller poems, Nocturnes, Preludes, and Etudes. We also find the names of
MM. Alard and Franchomme, while the vocalists
were Mlle. di Mondi (a niece of Pauline-Viardot),
and M. Roger, the tenor. So successful in every way
was this concert, that it was arranged that it should
be followed by another in the following month.
This, however, was not to be, owing to the outbreak
of the Revolution, which occurred only a week after
this first concert.

In 1847 Chopin published the last of his
works, the G minor Sonata for 'cello and piano
which we have already discussed. In April 1848 he
arrived in London, taking rooms in Bentinck Street,
which, after a few days, he left, going from there
to Dover Street. His works had preceded him here,
and he received in consequence an enthusiastic welcome. He went much into society, and played in
private a good deal. The first house at which he was
heard was that of Lady Blessington in Kensington,
which was a *rendezvous* of many distinguished
literary and musical celebrities. Later we hear of a
dinner at which, unfortunately, he was unable to be

present, given by Macready in his honour, to which were invited—Thackeray, Mrs. Proctor, Berlioz, and Sir Julius Benedict, while at the house of the Duchess of Sutherland the last-named musician played with Chopin a duet of Mozart's. Writing from Dover Street to his friend Gutmann in Paris, he says : 'Here I am at last, settled in this whirlpool of London. It is only a few days since I began to breathe, for it is only a few days since the sun showed itself. . . . Erard was charming; he sent me a piano. I have besides a Broadwood and a Pleyel, which makes three, but as yet I do not find time to play them. . . . A proposal has been made to me to play at the Philharmonic, but I would rather not. I shall apparently finish off, after playing at Court before the Queen, by giving a *matinée*, limited to a number of persons, at a private residence.'

He seems to have been charmed with the performances of Italian opera which were being given at this time at Covent Garden and Her Majesty's Theatres, and speaks in the most glowing terms of the singing of Madame Jenny Lind. In another letter he says: 'I have made Jenny Lind's personal acquaintance; when, a few days afterwards, I paid her a visit, she received me in the most amiable manner, and sent me an excellent "stall" for the opera.' The high opinion formed by Chopin of the singer was fully reciprocated by her, and she felt confident that he was not to blame in the rupture with Madame Sand; but as this is only the opinion of a woman who was very favourably impressed by Chopin, and who had only the advantage of the acquaintance of one of the parties, we can only take it for what it is worth. The private *matinées* given in London by Chopin were at the houses of Mrs. Sartoris (formerly Adelaide Kemble) in Eaton Place, and Lord Falmouth in St. James's Square, where he was assisted by Madame Viardot-Garcia, and Mlle. di Mondi.

In connection with these concerts we cannot do better than quote at length from Mr. Chorley's criticisms in the *Athenæum* at the time. Of the first, which took place on June 23d, he says:—' M. Chopin gave his audience yesterday week an hour and a half of such musical enjoyment as only great beauty, combined with great novelty, can command. We have had by turns this great player and the other great composer—we have been treated to the smooth, the splendid, the sentimental, the severe in style, upon the pianoforte one after the other. M. Chopin has proved to us that the instrument is capable of yet another "mode"—one in which delicacy, picturesqueness, elegance, and humour may be blended so as to produce that rare thing, a new delight. His treatment of the piano-forte is peculiar, and though we know that a system is not to be "explained in one word," we will mention a point or two so entirely novel, that even the distant amateur may in part conceive how, from such motions an original style of performance, and thence of composition, must inevitably result. Whereas other pianists have proceeded on the intention of equalising the power of the fingers, M. Chopin's plans are arranged so as to utilise their natural inequality of power, and, if carried out, provide varieties of expression not to be attained by those with whom evenness is the first excellence. Allied with this fancy are M. Chopin's peculiar mode of treating the scale and the shake, and his manner of sliding with one and the same finger from note to note, by way of producing a peculiar *legato*, and of passing the third over the fourth finger. All these innovations are art and part of his music as properly rendered, and as enacted by himself they charm by an ease and grace which, though super-fine, are totally distinct from affectation. After the "hammer and tongs" work on the pianoforte, to which we have of late years been accustomed, the delicacy of M. Chopin's tone, and the elasticity of his passages are delicious to the ear. He makes a free use of *tempo rubato*; leaning about within his bars more than any player we recollect, but still subject to a presiding sentiment of measure, such as presently habituates the ear to the liberties taken. In music not his own we happen to know he can be as staid as a metronome: while his mazurkas, etc., lose half their characteristic wildness if played without a certain freak and license—impossible to imitate, but irresistible if the player at all feel the music. This we have always fancied while reading

Chopin's works; we are now sure of it after

hearing him perform them himself. The pieces which M. Chopin gave at his *matinée* were— Notturni, Studies, *La Berceuse* (a delicate and lulling dream, with that most matter-of-fact substratum, a ground bass), two mazurkas, and two waltzes. Most of these might be called "gems," without misuse of the well worn symbol. Yet, if fantasy be allowed to characterise what is essentially fantastic, they are not so much gems as pearls— pearls in the changeful delicacy of their colour— in occasional irregularities of form, not destructive, however, of symmetry—pearls in their not being the products of health and strength. They will not displace and supersede other of our musical treasures, being different in tone and quality to any possessions we already enjoy; but inasmuch as art is not final, nor invention to be narrowed within the limits of experience, no musician, be he ever so straight-laced or severe—or vowed to his own school—can be indifferent to their exquisite and peculiar charm. It is to be hoped that M. Chopin will play again, and the next time some of his more developed compositions—such as Ballades,

Scherzi, etc., if not his Sonatas and Concerti. Few of his audience will be at all contented by a single hearing.' We quote at this length advisedly, as we cannot do better than accept the opinion of a musician and critic who had the good fortune to be present, especially when he is a critic of discernment, such as was Mr. Chorley. Speaking of the second *matinée* in the same journal, he says:—' M. Chopin played better at his second than at his first *matinée*—not with more delicacy (that could hardly be), but with more force and *brio*. Two among what may be called M. Chopin's more serious compositions were especially welcome to us—his Scherzo in B flat minor, and his Study in C sharp minor. The former we have long admired for its quaintness, grace, and remarkable variety—though it is guilty of a needlessly crude and hazardous modulation or two; the latter, again, is a masterpiece—original, expressive, and grand. No individual genius, we are inclined to theorise, is one-sided, however fondly the public is apt to fasten upon one characteristic, and disproportionately to foster its development; and if this crotchet be based on a sound harmony, M. Chopin could hardly be so intimately and exquisitely graceful as he is, if he could not on occasion be also grandiose.'

His physical weakness at this time was very great, —so great that he was quite unable to walk upstairs unassisted, and at Messrs. Broadwood's establishment, where it was necessary for him to ascend a flight of stairs in order to reach the room which contained the pianoforte intended for his use at the concert, two members of the firm actually carried him. What he must have felt and suffered at this time we can judge from his letters. Writing to his friend Grzymala, he says: 'I cannot be sadder than I am, for real joy I have not felt for a long time. Indeed, I feel nothing at all; I only vegetate, waiting patiently for my end.'

Shortly after this, at the invitation of some friends (Lord Torphichen, brother-in-law of Miss Stirling, his pupil), he left London for Scotland, and in Edinburgh he gave a concert at the Hopetoun Rooms, Queen Street,—Calder House, the residence of Lord Torphichen, being only some twelve miles from that city. For the concerts given by Chopin in Scotland

the piano was sent by Messrs. Broadwood to the care
of Mr. George Wood (of the firm of Cramer and
Co.), and the same eminent firm afterwards built
an iron-framed concert Grand specially for his use,
which he was destined never to play upon.   Mr.
A. J. Hipkins, who has ever been most courteous
and willing to throw what light he can upon Chopin's
second visit to the metropolis, very kindly sent me
a pamphlet written by himself, and full of interesting details connected with the history of the progress
of pianoforte construction.   It takes the form of a
'List of John Broadwood and Sons' exhibits at the
International Inventions Exhibition,' and can be
obtained from the firm.   On pages 10-13 is a description of the piano, specially constructed for
Chopin by Mr. Henry Fowler Broadwood, and others
which he also used.

Even less well than that of London does the climate
of Scotland seem to have suited the invalid.   Thus
does he describe his state :—' All the morning I
am quite incapable of doing anything, for no
sooner have I dressed myself than I feel so ex-
hausted that I must rest again.   After dinner I

have to sit for two hours with the gentlemen, to hear what they say, and to see what they drink. I am bored to death, and try to think of something else; after that I go to the drawing-room, where I need all my energy to rouse myself, for every one is anxious to hear me play.' In the latter part of August he accepted an engagement to play in Manchester, for which he was to receive £60. Of this concert there is a critique in the *Manchester Guardian* of August 30th, 1848, which, amongst other things, says:—'Chopin's music and style of performance partake of the same leading characteristics—refinement rather than vigour—subtle elaboration rather than simple comprehensiveness in composition—an elegant rapid touch, rather than a firm nervous grasp of the instrument. Both his compositions and playing appear to be the perfection of chamber music—fit to be associated with the most refined instrumental quartette and quartette playing—but wanting in breadth and obviousness of design and executive power to be effective in a large hall.'

This criticism, although not strictly correct of Chopin in his prime, was no doubt so of him at the time, for it was only to be expected that his executive power would suffer from the deplorable state of his health, and as the disease took firmer hold of him, so did his powers diminish. But, on the other hand, this lack of executive facility was fully compensated for by his exquisite *finesse*, which seemed to increase. Alboni sang at this concert. While staying in Manchester, Chopin was the guest of Mr. and Mrs. Schwabe, whose house he left, on or about the 7th September, for Glasgow. Here he gave a *matinée* some three weeks later. Although he pleased the Glasgow people, we cannot believe that at that time he was thoroughly 'understanded of them.' Nevertheless, one critic, speaking of his playing, showed his discernment by stating what was essentially true of Chopin, 'that his playing was more fitted for the home circle than the concert room.' On the 4th of October we find him giving a *soirée musicale* at the Hopetoun Rooms in Edinburgh. This was his third and last concert in Scotland, and, although surrounded by every kindness and comfort, neither the life nor climate was congenial to him. Of the Scotch people he wrote :—

'They are ugly, but, it would seem, good. As a compensation, there are charming and, apparently, mischièvous cattle, good milk, butter, and eggs.' While in a letter to his friend and pupil, Gutmann, he says: 'I drag myself from one lord to another, and from one duke to another. Everywhere I find, besides the greatest kindness and hospitality, excellent pianos and the choicest of pictures and books; there are also horses, dogs, interminable dinners, of which I avail myself little, and cellars, of which I avail myself even less. It is impossible to form an idea of all the elaborate comfort which reigns in these English mansions. . . . Cholera is coming; there is fog in London, and Paris is without a President. Therefore it matters not where I go to cough and suffocate.' This letter bears the address of his last abode in Scotland,—Calder House, near Edinburgh, and is dated October 16th, 1848. From here, some fourteen days later, Chopin returned to London, settling this time at 4 St. James's Place. Here we may leave him while we glance at his Waltzes, which, although we have left them to the last, are by no means least as regards their value;

indeed, as regards popularity, if that be taken as an earnest, they should, perhaps, be given the first place. In them we do not find the poetry of the Ballades or Etudes, nor do we find, to any great extent, the national colour of the Mazurkas; but, on the other hand, they are of exceptional value to us, if only because they demonstrate to a greater degree than any others of his works the bright and lightsome vein of his muse. Under Opus numbers, ranging from 18 to 70, we find thirteen Waltzes, of which ten were published during the composer's lifetime, besides which we have two more posthumous Waltzes without any Opus number. The first, Op. 18 in A flat, is a pure dance, the spirit of lightness prevailing. On arriving at the section in B flat minor, we get, perhaps, a somewhat more sombre shade, but it only lasts during these sixteen bars, and is greatly counteracted by the sprightliness of the *appoggiature* Notice the similarity between this section of the Waltz and the second part of the second Nocturne of Op. 32. Particularly exhilarating are the last sixty-four bars, commencing *poco a poco crescendo,* and working up in speed towards the end up to the last bar but twelve, when the repeated quaver figure gradually grows fainter and fainter, until the tonic chord *sf* is reached. The Op. 34 is, perhaps, more important from an æsthetic point of view, while it is certainly one of the most played, and, consequently, most abused of any. The second of the same Opus is not so important, and is in a much more melancholy vein. No. 1 of Op. 64 in D flat has obtained the name of the *Valse du Petit Chien*, owing to Chopin having composed it, as illustrative of the frantic efforts of Madame Sand's little dog to succeed in catching its own tail. The story goes, that one evening, as they were watching the proceeding, Madame Sand suggested it to Chopin for musical treatment, and he at once sat down to the piano and improvised this Waltz in D flat.

No. 2 of this Opus is one of the most delightful. It has an additional charm from its minor tonality, and especially delicate is the *più mosso* portion in C sharp minor. Then what a beautiful contrast we get from the enharmonic change into D flat major, with its passionate and flowing melody, one of the most voluptuous pieces Chopin has written. In

No. 3 of the Opus there is a falling off in material, although its treatment is replete with delicacy. Decidedly the most notable portion is that in C major in the middle section. This is most virile, and almost reminds us of that turn of the composer's genius which is exemplified in the Polonaises.

In the remaining Waltzes, published after his death, there is neither much that is new, nor is their value to be compared with those we have named. Perhaps the best of the posthumous Waltzes is No. 3 of Op. 70, in G flat, which is remarkable for its easy writing, and the intense amount of movement and life contained in it. Inasmuch as these works are, for the most part, essentially of the ball-room, they are not to be put on a similar level as, for example, the Ballades or Preludes; but, on the other hand, they are as much superior to all other music of the kind as the Scherzo in B flat minor and the Ballade in G minor, for instance, are superior to them. Throughout they are distinguished by an elegance and exquisite clarity which make them as nearly as possible perfect.

CHAPTER XIV

In November 1848 Chopin wrote the following letter
to his friend Grzymala :—

'My dearest Friend,—For the past eighteen days—that
is, since my arrival in London—I have been ill, and have suffered from such a severe cold in my head (together with headache, difficulty in breathing), in fact, all my bad symptoms, that
I have not been able to get out of doors.   The doctor sees me
daily, and has so far succeeded in restoring me, that yesterday
I was able to take part in the Polish concert and ball,
returning home, however, as soon as ever I was able to leave.
Throughout the night I got no sleep, and suffered, besides my
cough and asthma, from the most violent headache.   So far
the fog has not been so very bad, and I have been able to
open the windows of my rooms, notwithstanding the intense
cold.   I am now living at 4 St. James's Street, and have for
my regular daily visitors, the excellent Szulczewski, Broadwood, Mrs. Erskine, who followed me here in company with
Mr. Stirling, and especially Prince Alexander and his wife.
. . . I am not yet able to return to Paris, although I am
always thinking of how I can manage to get there.   In these
apartments, which for an ordinarily healthy man would be
well enough, I cannot remain, although the situation is good,

and they are not dear (four and a half guineas a week), they
are close to those of Lord Stuart, who has only just left me.
I shall probably take up my quarters with him, as his rooms
are much larger, and in them I shall be able to breathe more
freely. Nevertheless, you might inquire, please, whether there
are not somewhere on the Boulevards, in the neighbourhood
of the Rue de la Paix, or the Rue Royale, apartments to be
had on the first floor, with windows facing the south, or even
in the Rue des Mathurins, but not in the Rue Godot, or any
such gloomy narrow street. . . . . Why I should trouble
you with all this I do not know, for I really do not care
about anything. Although I do not think I ever cursed any
one before, I am now so overcome by the very weariness of
life, that I am ready to curse Lucrezia.[1] But she suffers
also, the more so, as every day she grows older in her
wickedness. Alas! everything is going wrong; but it is no
use troubling about me; I cannot be more wretched than I
am, and there is no chance of my being less so. I await
patiently the end. If you find suitable apartments, let me
know at once, but do not, until then, give up the old ones.
—Ever yours,   FREDERIC.'

The abject despondency of this letter is truly
affecting. The concert to which he refers in connection with the Polish ball, seems only to have been a
very secondary portion of the whole entertainment,
and he was decidedly ill-advised to have taken part

---

[1] He evidently refers to George Sand.

in it, for, as Mr. Hueffer very truly says, 'The people, hot from dancing, who went into the room where he played, were but little in the humour to pay attention, and only anxious to return to their amusement.' Moreover, no matter how unreservedly they had given themselves up to it, the result could not have been but disappointing, as he was in such a state of exhaustion as to be physically incapable of interpreting his artistic meaning.   Although, as we have seen from his last letter to Grzymala in November, Chopin was then anxious to return to Paris, he did not leave London until the following January.   The last letter he wrote to this friend in English soil contains the news of his intended departure :—' To-day I have been down almost the whole day, but on Thursday I am to leave this terrible London.   I shall probably sleep on Thursday night at Boulogne, but shall hope on the night following to be in my bed in the Place d'Orleans. In addition to my other ailments, I have now got neuralgia.   Tell Madame Etienne to spare no pains to make the place warm and comfortable when I arrive; also tell Pleyel to send me a piano on Thursday, and please see that some violets be bought, so that there may be a nice fragrance in the room. I should like, also, to find some books of poetry in my bedroom, as I shall in all probability be confined therein for some time. On Friday evening, then, you may expect me in Paris; a day longer here, and I should go mad or die. My Scotch lady friends are good, but tiresome; they have so attached themselves to me that I find it impossible to get rid of them. Have all the rooms well warmed and dusted—perhaps I may get well again.'

How thoroughly typical of the consumptive patient is the last sentence. It is one of the many merciful provisions of Providence that, up to the very last, hope never dies within them. And it is something to be thankful for that this hope was never absent in Chopin's case. Up to the very end he looked for a future in this world. It is more than probable that his sojourn amidst us during that winter season did not a little to aggravate the fell disease, while we can take it for certain that, to the cruel desertion of him by the woman on whom he had pinned his faith, is due the hastening of the end. Chopin was now no longer able to teach, and was obliged to maintain, almost entirely, a recumbent position. To add to his troubles he was at the same time dealt a heavy blow by the death of his physician, Dr. Molin, in whom he placed great confidence, and to whom he looked as his support. Says Liszt:—'He felt his loss keenly—nay, it brought a profound discouragement with it . . . he persuaded himself that no one could replace the trusted physician, and he had no confidence in any other. Dissatisfied with them all, without any hope from their skill, he changed them constantly, and a kind of superstitious depression seized him.' He now learned that his dear friend Titus Woyciechowski was at Ostend; to him he writes:—'Nothing but my being so severely ill as I am should prevent me from hastening to you at Ostend; nevertheless I trust that, by the goodness of God, you may be permitted to come to me. The doctors will not allow me to travel. I am confined to my room, and am drinking Pyrenean water, but your presence would do me more good than all these medicines.' This letter was written towards the end of August from the Place d'Orleans, but from these rooms he was removed to more open and suitable quarters in the Rue Chaillot. Ever improvident, the money which he had made in England had gone, and he himself knew not how. His friends were in despair for him, and at a loss how to overcome this very substantial difficulty. Franchomme, who had always advised him in money matters, took counsel with some few of the composer's intimates, and ultimately decided to let his staunch friend and pupil, Miss Stirling, know of her master's deplorable position. And to her credit be it said that no sooner was she made aware of the facts of the case, than she immediately responded in the shape of a sum of francs—25,000. Concerning her generosity all his biographers are agreed, but with respect to the circumstances surrounding it there are several stories told. The correct one is probably that told by Professor Niecks, who states that it was Madame Rubio, also a pupil of Chopin's, who was the one to acquaint Miss Stirling with the facts of the case, and that she was amazed at the news, having some short time previously sent her master 25,000 francs, which she addressed and sealed in a shop, in order that he should be ignorant of the identity of the sender.

Also, that the packet was eventually discovered in a clock in the room of the *portière*, who having forgotten to hand it in the first place to Chopin, feared to do so afterwards, and allowed it to remain there. Madame Rubio avers that Chopin kept only 1000 francs of the money, and returned the rest to Miss Stirling, while Franchomme's version is that the master retained 12,000 francs. At all events, of the great generosity of his pupil there can be no question. Perhaps we should state, for what it is worth, that there had been rumours that this lady was deeply enamoured of her master, and that they were about to be married; but there was absolutely no foundation for such a report, and we can only treat it as idle gossip. .

Nor was this the only example of friendliness held out to Chopin in his time of need. The apartments in the Rue Chaillot were considerably more expensive than those in the Place d'Orleans; but this was carefully kept from the invalid by those around him, as was also the fact that his friend, the Comtesse Obreskoff, paid one-half of the rent. From a letter to Franchomme we see that even another change became necessary, for he says:—' I am less well rather than better. MM. Cruveillé, Louis, and Blache have had a consultation, and have come to the conclusion that I ought not to travel, but only to take lodgings in the south and remain in Paris. After much seeking, very dear apartments, combining all the necessary conditions, have been found in the Place Vendôme, No. 12.' Accordingly, after a stay of only six weeks in the Rue Chaillot, we find him located in the Place Vendôme.

His relations in Poland had now to be apprised of his condition, and his sister, Madame Louisa Jedrzejewicz, accompanied by her husband and daughter, left Poland for Paris. Once beside him, his sister never left him for a moment. His dearest friend and pupil, Gutmann, was also now constantly with him, and both friend and sister felt that the end was not far off. On the 15th October his friend, the Comtesse Delphine Potocka, arrived in Paris, having hastened from Nice, where she was at the time, directly she heard of the master's illness. No sooner was he made aware of her presence than he implored her to sing to him. Says Liszt: ' Who could have ventured to oppose his wish? The piano was rolled to the door of his chamber, while with sobs in her voice and tears streaming down her cheeks his gifted countrywoman sang. She sang that famous Canticle to the Virgin, which, it is said, once saved the life of Stradella. "How beautiful it is!" he exclaimed. "My God, how very beautiful! Again, again!" Though overwhelmed with emotion, the countess had the noble courage to comply with the last wish of a friend and compatriot: she again took a seat at the piano, and sang a hymn from Marcello. Chopin now feeling worse; everybody was seized with fright; by a spontaneous impulse all who were present threw themselves upon their knees—no one ventured to speak; the sacred silence was only broken by the voice of the singer floating like a melody from heaven, above the sighs and sobs which formed its mournful earth accompaniment.' Since the publication of Professor Niecks's biography, considerable doubt must be felt as to the accuracy of Liszt's statement touching upon what the lady sang; for he states that 'Gutmann positively asserted that she sang a psalm by Marcello, and an air by Pergolesi, while Franchomme insisted on her having sung an air from Bellini's *Beatrice di Tenda*, and that only once, and nothing else.' We know that both the authors of these statements were present, whereas Liszt was not; but while that leaves no doubt as to the incorrectness of the Abbé in this particular, it does not help us in deciding between the relative statements of the two witnesses. This, of course, is impossible, as there is nothing whatever to guide us to a trustworthy decision. To Professor Niecks, also, do we owe much of interest concerning these last hours of the master, inasmuch as he has brought to light much new testimony of a further witness, M. Gavard, who relates how, on the day following, Chopin called around him those friends who were with him in his apartment. To the Princess Czartoryska and Mlle. Gavard, he said: 'You will play together; you will think of me, and I shall listen to you.' Beckoning to Franchomme, he said to the princess, 'I recommend Franchomme to you; you will play Mozart together, and I shall listen to you!'

And all this time, the reader may ask, 'Where was

the woman who had sworn that he should die in no arms but hers? Was she so far lost to all human feeling and decency as not even to appear to show some interest in the man to whom she had professed so much, and from whom life was now so rapidly passing?' On this point, again, the evidence left to us is conflicting, so contradictory are the versions of those upon whom we are dependent. M. Gavard asserts that a certain lady, whom he calls Madame M., came in the name of George Sand to inquire after Chopin's health. Gutmann differs from him widely. 'George Sand,' he says, 'came herself to the landing of the staircase, and desired to be allowed to see Chopin, but that he strongly advised her against such a course, deeming it liable to disastrously affect the patient.' In either case the result was the same as regards Chopin, for he was kept in complete ignorance of any action on the part of Madame Sand. How keenly he felt her desertion is shown by the fact that, only two days before his death, in speaking of her to Franchomme, he said: '*Elle m'avait dit que je ne mourrais que dans ses bras.*' How well he was cared for, and how much devotion and tenderness were lavished upon him, we can judge from another letter of M. Gavard, quoted by Professor Niecks, in which he says:—'In the back room lay the poor sufferer, tormented by fits of breathlessness, and only sitting in bed resting in the arms of a friend could he procure air for his oppressed lungs. It was Gutmann, the strongest amongst us, who knew best how to manage the patient, and who mostly thus supported him. At the head of his bed sat the Princess Czartoryska: she never left him, guessing his most secret wishes, nursing him like a Sister of Mercy with a serene countenance which did not betray her deep sorrow. Other friends gave a helping hand or relieved her,— everyone according to his power; but most of them stayed in the two adjoining rooms. Everyone had assumed a part; everyone helped as much as he could—one ran to the doctor's, to the apothecary; another introduced the persons asked for; a third shut the door on the intruders.'

But, alas! the door was not to be shut upon the greatest of all intruders, and on the evening of the 16th October the Abbé Alexander Jelowicki, the

Polish priest, was sent for, as Chopin, saying that he had not confessed for many years, wished to do so now. After the confession was over, and the absolution pronounced, Chopin, embracing his confessor, exclaimed, 'Thanks! thanks to you, I shall not now die like a pig.' The same evening two doctors examined him. His difficulty in breathing now seemed intense: but on being asked whether he still suffered, he replied, 'No longer.' His face had already assumed the pure serenity of death, and every minute was expected to be the last. Just before the end—at two o'clock on the morning of the 17th—he drank some wine handed to him by Gutmann, who held the glass to his lips. *'Cher ami!'* he said, and, kissing his faithful pupil's hand, he died. 'He died as he had lived,' says Liszt, 'in loving.'

Knowing how great a lover of flowers he had been, the floral tributes sent by his friends were many and beautiful. 'He seemed to repose in a bed of roses,' says Liszt. The press was unanimous in its expression of sorrow on the great loss sustained by art in the death of the master. The funeral, owing to the elaborate preparations which were made in connection with it, did not take place until the 30th of October. The service was held at the Madeleine, and Mozart's Requiem was performed, for the better execution of which an exception was made, and female singers were allowed to take part in the rendering. For a further account of the ceremony, we shall quote from the notice which appeared in the *Musical World* of November 10th, 1849 :—'The ceremony, which took place on Tuesday (the 30th ult.) at noon in the Church of the Madeleine, was one of the most imposing we ever remember to have witnessed. The great door of the church was hung with black curtains, with the initials of the deceased, " F. C.," emblazoned in silver. . . . At noon the service began. The orchestra and chorus (both from the Conservatoire, with M. Gérard as conductor), and the principal singers (Madame Viardot-Garcia, Madame Castellan, Signor Lablache, and M. Alexis Dupont) were placed at the extreme end of the church, a black drapery concealing them from view. When the service commenced the drapery was partially withdrawn, and exposed the male executants to view, concealing the women, whose presence, being uncanonical, was being felt, not seen. A solemn March was then struck up by the band, during the performance of which the coffin, containing the body of the deceased, was slowly carried up the middle of the nave. . . The March that accompanied the body to the mausoleum was Chopin's own composition from his first piano-forte Sonata,[1] instrumented for the orchestra by M. Henri Reber. During the ceremony, M. Lefébure-Wély, organist of the Madeleine, performed two of Chopin's Preludes upon the organ.[2] . . . After the service, M. Wély played a Voluntary, introducing themes from Chopin's compositions, while the crowd dispersed with decorous gravity. The coffin was then carried from the church, all along the Boulevards, to the cemetery of Père-Lachaise—a distance of three miles, at least—Meyerbeer and the other chief mourners, who held the cords, walking bareheaded. . . . At Père-Lachaise, in one of the most secluded spots near the tombs of Habeneck and Marie Milanollo, the coffin was deposited in a newly-made grave. . . . The ceremony was performed in silence.'

[1] The Op. 35, the first then published.   [2] Nos. 4 and 6.

We also gather from other authorities that the number of people assembled in the Madeleine amounted to some three thousand, all of whom were present by special invitation. Amongst the pall-bearers were Princes Adam and Alexander Czartoryski, Eugène Delacroix, Meyerbeer, Franchomme, and Gutmann; while, perhaps, the names of Bellini, Cherubini, Boieldieu, and Grétry, whose graves were also in close proximity, are more important than those quoted in the notice above given.

It has been frequently stated that Chopin expressed a wish to be buried beside Bellini, but this, according to Gutmann, was not so. The same authority also denies that his master desired the performance of Mozart's Requiem at his funeral. We should not omit to state that the Polish earth given to the young musician on quitting his native land, some nineteen years before, by his friends, was buried with him, being sprinkled over the coffin as it was lowered into the grave, and that his heart was taken to, and preserved in, the Holy Cross Church at Warsaw.

The visitor to Père-Lachaise will now find his rest-

ing-place marked by a handsome monument, erected
by subscription, and executed by M. Clesinger, whom
we know as the husband of Madame Sand's daughter
Solange.   It consists of a pedestal, which supports
a mourning muse, with a lyre in her hand; on the
front of the pedestal is a medallion.   It was unveiled
on the first anniversary of Chopin's death, and bears
the inscription: 'Frederic Chopin, né en Pologne à
Zelazowa Wola, près de Varsovie: Fils d'un émigré
français, marié à Mlle. Krzyzanowska, fille d'un
gentilhomme Polonais.'

Thus was the last earthly tribute paid to one who,
if he laboured not in the larger fields of his art, did,
in his exquisite miniatures, leave us so much of his
own personality as to form an ever-living monument
of the genius and the man.

CONCLUSION

Having followed poor Chopin to his last resting
place, little remains for us to do, save to glance at
those compositions of which we have not yet spoken.
Foremost amongst these are the Berceuse, Op. 57;
and the Barcarolle, Op. 60. Both are masterpieces
in their way, and both are—as their Opus numbers
would lead us to expect—in the master's later manner.
The basis of the Berceuse is the rocking figure for
the left hand. Upon this the whole of the super-
structure is built. The phrase, which is the very
essence of dreaminess, consists simply of tonic and
dominant harmony, and continues throughout the

piece, with the exception of the twelfth and thirteenth
bars, in which it is supplanted for the moment by

that of the sub-dominant. The rhythm also is the same, never differing from that which we have illustrated. Here is the soothsome melody upon which Chopin brings to bear all his infinite variety and ingenuity of workmanship :—

The lavish and minute elaboration of this theme quite defies all attempts at description, yet never for one moment does it frustrate the composer's intention. We can readily imagine the child being rocked to sleep in the arms of its nurse, and the last eight bars would even seem to depict how she herself, after having soothed her charge, was obliged to succumb to the influence of the melody. Never was music written more happily bearing out its title.

In the Barcarolle we have, perhaps, the only successful attempt by Chopin at what is commonly called local colour. After three bars of introduction, the accompanying theme in the bass is introduced, and although its use is not continuous, as was the case in the Berceuse, it may be said to form the whole basis of the Cantilena. The principal theme is announced after two bars of the accompaniment figures played aloud, and ten bars later is brought to a full close on the dominant C sharp. Then follows an exquisite little codetta, which is a few bars later repeated in the key of the sub-dominant. We then have the original theme in F sharp slightly elaborated, and followed in turn by the codetta in the tonic key. At the *poco più mosso* are four bars modulating from F sharp to A minor, in which latter key we have an episode. This portion of the work affords an artistic contrast to the matter both preceding and following it. Mr. Niecks quotes a flowery description by Tausig of the Barcarolle, which, he says, the virtuoso imagined to be descriptive of two lovers in a gondola. That a duologue is taking place, he assumes to be evident from the use of the thirds and sixths, and the dualism which is maintained throughout. At the modulation to C sharp, which occurs in the interlude leading from the tributary of the A major episode to the initial theme in F sharp, he conjures up the picture of the two lovers embracing, which he takes to be the more emphasised by the marking of the passage *dolce sfogata*—softly breathed-out. The picture is a pretty one, and there can be no doubt that some such idea was in the composer's mind at the time he wrote it. Nevertheless, no word-picture can convey the many subtleties which the piece contains. We can only get an adequate idea of them by listening to its perfect interpretation. It is essentially a piece which impresses at a first hearing. The only works now remaining which we propose to consider, are the Rondo, Op. 73; and the Seventeen Polish Songs, Op. 74,—both posthumous publications. The Rondo for two pianofortes is in C major, and in the master's early manner. It is essentially a 'showy' composition, and affords much opportunity for the display of mechanical dexterity. The first piano opens with an introductory, four bars of ascending semiquaver figures, to which the second instrument replies with four bars of *sostenuto* chords. The leading theme of the Rondo is brilliant, and the musical matter equally divided between the two instruments. It is well contrasted with the second theme in A minor, which is much more pensive in character. This second theme affords much scope for brilliant accompaniment by the other instrument, a fact which is not lost sight of by the composer, and of which he takes the fullest advantage, so much so, that the ornamental passage work forms the most interesting feature of the piece, which is totally lacking in that originality of thought and design which is so abundant in Chopin's later efforts. The work is seldom heard in public now, and the only important performance of it which we can call to mind took place at Messrs. Chappell's popular concert on January 15th, 1877, when it was admirably played by Miss Agnes Zimmermann and Mlle. Marie Krebs. It can in no way be considered as fairly representative of its composer.

Under Op. number 74 were published by Julius Fontana the only songs Chopin wrote. The Opus contains seventeen Polish songs composed from 1824-1844, to words supplied chiefly by the poets Mickiewicz and Witwicki. The melodies are essentially national, and are seldom subjected by the composer to anything in the way of development. Those which have most claim in this direction, and which, to our mind, form the most interesting numbers of the collection, are Nos. 3, 6, 12, and 16. Especially noticeable in some of these is a decided influence of Bellini, while in others there is present much that is in common with the German *lied*. On contemplating them we have no difficulty in comprehending Schumann, when he said that Chopin, in his melodies, leant sometimes over Germany towards Italy. The *Andantino espressivo* of No. 6, *Mir aus den Blicken*, might have been written by Bellini, so much does it contain that is reminiscent of him. No. 3 is exquisitely sad. Note in it the following bar,* the effect of which strikes the English ear as decidedly peculiar.

There are not wanting in these vocal compositions reminiscences of some of the instrumental works.

As prominent examples of this, note the introductory bars to Nos. 1 and 14. Specially illustrative of the 'national' detail in them is the use of the augmented fourth degree of the scale—*vide* bar 9 in No. 2, and the interlude in No. 4; while amongst those which are national, rather in the spirit than the letter, we should mention Nos. 2, 4, 7, 13, and 17. The last of these has been called *Poland's dirge.*

Karasowski describes how Chopin, in his youth, imbibed these Polish national melodies:—'When on an excursion with his father to the suburbs, or spending his holidays in the country, he always listened attentively to the song of the reaper, and the tune of the peasant fiddler, fixing in his memory and delighting to idealise those frequently original and expressive melodies. He often wondered who was the creator of the beautiful melodies interwoven in the Mazurkas, Cracoviennes, and Polonaises, and how the Polish peasants learnt to sing and play the violin with such purity. No one could give him any information. Indeed, both the words and melodies of these songs are the creation of several minds. An artless spontaneous melody poured forth by one person is altered and perhaps improved by another, and so passes from mouth to mouth till finally it becomes a possession of the people. Slavonic folk-songs differ greatly from the Germanic ; they are historical records of the feelings, customs, and character of the people.'

We have now contemplated all the more important works from Chopin's pen, and of the work of all the greater masters of music none are more conflicting. It would be going too far to assert that the primary qualities of his genius were evenly balanced with his primary faults. Yet what is this dissatisfaction which we feel? In the breadth and brilliance of his conception, the energy and sweep of his imagination, his power of dealing with the subtleties of music he is unsurpassed amongst the masters of his art. Thoroughly subjective, his work is saturate in his own personality. He stands alone amongst musicians, and his compositions are a distinct musical literature in themselves. Yet over all is the fragrance, not of nature, but of the hot-house. Even his Ballades and his Scherzos, which we may term the 'fine-flower' of his genius, have not escaped its influence. Moreover, in much of his work his mannerisms are discomfortably glaring, and yet, while he is frequently artificial, he has the wonderful faculty of never appearing to be so. Of all his compositions, the most characteristic and individual are those in which he has given his invention full swing, and allowed his fancy to play its maddest pranks. His empire is essentially over the imagination and the passions, and he is the very antipodes of those artists —pensive and sedately self-contained—such as were, for instance, Beethoven and Mendelssohn. Were it not for Berlioz we might fitly call Frederic Chopin the 'Hugo of music,' just as Delacroix was called the 'Hugo of painting.' But now we come to the strangest point of all, for with his ideas, his theories of art, his natural bent, one and all, in sympathy with romanticism, the works of such leaders of the romantic school as Berlioz and Schumann were in many instances repugnant to him, and while he himself threw off all the fetters of classicism, his god was Mozart! When we know this, it is easy to understand that the compositions of Franz Liszt found little favour in his eyes. For there is a distinction even amongst the greatest romanticists. As

well compare Liszt with Schumann, as Victor Hugo
with Alfred de Musset. Liszt 'wandered' without
reason, Chopin, when he did wander, had generally, if
not reason, justification for it. Liszt,—at all events
as regards composition,—was a *poseur*; a man who,
having taken up a certain attitude in his art, was
determined to stick to it at all costs—a man who
affected musical composition, and the best of whose
pianoforte compositions can only be deemed of worth
as tending to develop the technique of the player. A
truly wonderful interpreter and adapter of other
men's creations, but no creator. Chopin was, like
Heine, 'a man angry until death with the shallow
forms and conventionalities possessed no longer of
any spiritual import,' and, in common with Heine, he
has demonstrated in his work a formal fragmentari-
ness which is by no means wholly distinct from
completeness. His aim was ever to write music
capable of expressing a definite emotion. This in itself, when carried to any great extent, is sufficient to
lead to the loss of the highest beauty of 'form,' for
the obvious reason that the means to this emotional
colouring,—such as the use of vivid harmonies,

numerous chromatic and enharmonic modulations, and a consequent shifting tonality,—are in themselves opposed to the laws of regular 'form.' In a word, his music is *poetic* as opposed to *tonic*. This poetic emotional expression, and the artistic sense of tonic beauty are respectively the two distinct ingredients of the romantic and the classic schools, and it seems to us that any music which displays great achievement in either direction justifies its existence, and that the art itself is the gainer thereby. Nevertheless, it is when we get these two essentials combined in artistic unison that the highest attainment of music is realised. And this we may safely say we do get —if only in isolated instances—in the music of Frederic Chopin. It is safe to say that there will be always enthusiastic upholders of both the classic and romantic schools; but that the partisans of the respective schools should—as an American critic has recently said—proceed as if the matter were to be settled by the 'Marquis of Queensberry' rules is surely unnecessary and ridiculous. We cannot believe that the true enthusiast in art is so egotistical and stubborn as not to admit good music when he hears

it, no matter to what school it may belong. The only
good which we can see likely to arise from such
discussions is that interest in the art is perhaps
stimulated thereby.   Take, for instance, what is
commonly called 'Programme-music.' This has of
late given rise to an enormous amount of arguing for
and against its existence.   There are some people who
deny the existence of music from which they cannot
obtain a 'clear definition.'   There are others who say
that to expect such a thing is absurd—that the
sphere of music is in sensuous perception, while the
sphere of poetry is in intelligence.   There is, of course,
much to be said on both sides, and as regards
Frederic Chopin, he undoubtedly did write much
that can be called Programme-music ; but with
this distinction—that he did not make it a *sine
qua non* that his listeners should follow his 'programme.'   His nature was so subjective that his
musical utterances were for the most part illustrative
of definite emotions and events in his mind at the
time.   Does this necessarily detract from the value of
his work as music *per se* ? Undoubtedly, as we have
before said, a much higher meaning and fuller com-

prehension, and consequently a deeper artistic appreciation, is there for him who can find the key to their emotional basis. But apart from that altogether, they are still works of art. It is in his intensity of feeling that the magic of his music lies, and this, which is human nature, must make itself felt by all, whether classicist or romanticist. He had faults, no doubt, and we trust we have not shrunk from pointing out such as seemed to us to mar in any way the æsthetic effect of his work. But, on the other hand, the beauties to be noticed in his works are innumerable. And whatever may be said for or against his artistic methods, the fact remains that he left the world richer by far than he found it.

LIST OF CHOPIN'S PUBLISHED WORKS.

I.—Those with Opus Number Published during his Lifetime.

Opus No.	Date of Publication.	Title.	Key.	Dedication.
1	1825	Rondo for pianoforte	C minor	Madame de Linde
2	1830	Variations for pianoforte, with orchestral accompaniment on *La ci dar-em la mano*	B major	M. Woyciechowski
3	1833	Introduction and Polonaise for pianoforte and violoncello	C major	M. Joseph Merk
5	1827	Rondo à la Mazurka	F major	Mlle. la Comtesse Alexandrine de Moriolles
6	1832	Four Mazurkas for pianoforte	F sharp minor C sharp minor E major E flat major	Mlle. la Comtesse Pauline Plater
7	1832	Five Mazurkas for pianoforte	B major A minor F minor A flat major C major	M. Johns
8	1833	First Trio for pianoforte, violin, and violoncello	G minor	Prince Antoine Radziwill
9	1833	Three Nocturnes	B flat minor E flat major B major	Mme. Camille Pleyel
10	1833	Twelve Grand Studies	C major A minor E major C sharp minor G flat major E flat minor	M. Franz Liszt

U

Opus No.	Date of Publication.	Title.	Key.	Dedication.
10	1833	Twelve Grand Studies—*continued*	C major F major F minor A flat major E flat major C minor	M. Franz Liszt
11	1833	Grand Concerto for pianoforte and orchestra	E minor	M. Fr. Kalkbrenner
12	1833	Variations for pianoforte on the favourite Rondo of Hérold *Je vends des Scapulaires*	B major	Miss Emma Horsford
13	1834	Grand Fantasia on Polish Airs for piano and orchestra	A major	Mr. F. P. Pixis
14	1834	Krakowiak, Grand Concert Rondo for piano and orchestra	F major	Mme. la Princesse Adam Czartoryska
15	1834	Three Nocturnes	F major F sharp major G minor	M. Ferd. Hiller
16	1834	Rondo for pianoforte	E flat major	Mlle. Caroline Hartmann
17	1834	Four Mazurkas for pianoforte	B flat major E minor A flat major A minor	Mme. Lina Freppa
18	1834	Grand Waltz for pianoforte	E flat major	Miss Laura Horsford
19	1834	Bolero for pianoforte	C major	Mlle. la Comtesse E. de Flahault
20	1835	First Scherzo for pianoforte	B minor	Mr. T. Albrecht
21	1836	Second Concerto for pianoforte and orchestra	F minor	Mme. la Comtesse Delphine Potocka
22	1836	Grand Polonaise preceded by *Andante spianato*	E flat major	Mme. la Baronne d'Est
23	1836	Ballade for pianoforte	G minor	Baron Stockhausen
24	1835	Four Mazurkas for pianoforte	G minor C major A flat major B minor	M. le Comte de Perthuis

Opus No.	Date of Publication.	Title.	Key.	Dedication.
25	1837	Twelve Studies	A flat major F minor F major A minor E minor G sharp minor C sharp minor D flat major G flat major B minor A minor C minor	Mme. la Comtesse d'Agoult
26	1836	Two Polonaises for pianoforte	C sharp minor E flat minor	M. J. Dessauer
27	1836	Two Nocturnes for pianoforte	C sharp minor D flat major	Mme. la Comtesse d'Appony
28	1836	Twenty-four Preludes for pianoforte	...	M. Camille Pleyel (in German edition to Mr. J. C. Kessler)
29	1838	Impromptu for pianoforte	A flat major	Mlle. la Comtesse de Lobau
30	1834	Four Mazurkas for pianoforte	C minor B minor D flat major C sharp minor	Mme. la Princesse de Würtemberg
31	1838	Second Scherzo for pianoforte	B flat minor	Mlle. la Comtesse Adele de Fürstenstein
32	1837	Two Nocturnes for pianoforte	B major A flat major	Mme. la Baronne de Billing
33	1838	Four Mazurkas for pianoforte	G sharp minor D major C major B minor	Mlle. la Comtesse Mostowska
34	1838	Three Waltzes for pianoforte	A flat major to A minor to F major to	Mlle. de Thun-Hohenstein Mme. G. d'Ivri Mlle. A. d'Eichthal
35	1840	Sonata for pianoforte	B flat minor	...
36	1840	Second Impromptu for pianoforte	F sharp major	...
37	1840	Two Nocturnes for pianoforte	G minor G major	...
38	1840	Second Ballade for pianoforte	F major	M. Robert Schumann

Opus No.	Date of Publication.	Title.	Key.	Dedication.
39	1840	Third Scherzo for pianoforte	C sharp minor	M. A. Gutmann
40	1840	Two Polonaises for pianoforte	A major C minor	M. J. Fontana
41	1840	Four Mazurkas for pianoforte	C sharp minor E minor B major A flat major	M. E. Witwicki
42	1840	Waltz for pianoforte	A flat major	...
43	1841	Tarentella for pianoforte	A flat major	...
44	1841	Polonaise for pianoforte	F sharp minor	Mme. la Princesse Charles de Beauvau
45	1841	Prélude for pianoforte	C sharp minor	Mlle. la Princesse ElizabethCzernicheff
46	1842	Concert Allegro for pianoforte	A major	Mlle. F. Müller
47	1842	Third Ballade for pianoforte	A flat major	Mlle. P. de Noailles
48	1842	Two Nocturnes for pianoforte	C minor F sharp minor	Mlle. L. Duperré
49	1842	Fantasia for pianoforte	F minor	Mme. la Princesse C. de Souzzo
50	1842	Three Mazurkas for pianoforte	G major A flat major C sharp minor	M. Léon Szmitkowski
51	1843	Allegro Vivace, Third Impromptu for pianoforte	G flat major	Mme. la Comtesse Esterhazy
52	1843	Fourth Ballade for the pianoforte	F minor	Mme. la Baronne C. de Rothschild
53	1843	Eighth Polonaise for the pianoforte	A flat major	M. A. Leo
54	1843	Fourth Scherzo for the pianoforte	E major	Mlle. J. de Caraman
55	1844	Two Nocturnes for the pianoforte	F minor E flat major	Mlle. J. W. Stirling
56	1844	Three Mazurkas for the pianoforte	B major C major C minor	Mlle. C. Maberly
57	1845	Berceuse for pianoforte	D flat major	Mlle. Elise Gavard
58	1845	Sonata for the pianoforte	B minor	Mme. la Comtesse E. de Perthuis
59	1846	Three Mazurkas for pianoforte	A minor A flat major F sharp minor	...

Opus No.	Date of Publi- cation.	Title.	Key.	Dedication.
60	1846	Barcarolle for the piano- forte	F sharp minor	Mme. la Baronne Stockhausen
61	1846	Polonaise Fantasia for the pianoforte	A flat major	Mme. A. Veyret
62	1846	Two Nocturnes for the pianoforte	B major E major	Mlle. R. de Köuneritz
63	1847	Three Mazurkas for the pianoforte	B major F minor C sharp minor	Mme. la Comtesse Czosnowska
64	1847	Three Waltzes for the pianoforte	D flat major C sharp minor A flat major	Mme. la Comtesse Potocka Mme. la Baronne de Rothschild Mme. la Baronne Bronicka
65	1847	Sonata for pianoforte and violoncello	G minor	M. A. Franchomme

---

II.—THOSE PUBLISHED WITHOUT OPUS NUMBER DURING THE COMPOSER'S LIFE.

Date.	Title.	Key.
1833	Grand Duet Concertante for pianoforte and violon- cello, on themes from *Robert the Devil*	E major
1840	Three Studies for the pianoforte	F minor A flat major D flat major
1841	Variations on Bellini's March from *I Puritani*	E major
1842	Mazurka for pianoforte	A minor

U 2

III.—THOSE PUBLISHED POSTHUMOUSLY WITH OPUS NUMBER.

Opus.	Date of Composition.	Date of Publication.	Title.	Key.
4	1828	1851	Sonata for pianoforte	C minor
66	1834	1855	Fantasia-Impromptu for pianoforte	C sharp minor
67	1835	1855	Four Mazurkas for pianoforte	G major
	1849	,,	... ...	G minor
	1835	,,	... ...	C major
	1846	,,	... ...	A minor
68	1830	1855	Four Mazurkas for pianoforte	C major
	1827	,,	... ...	A minor
	1830	,,	... ...	F major
	1849	,,	... ...	F minor
69	1836	1855	Two Waltzes for pianoforte	F minor
	1829	,,	... ...	B minor
70	1835	1855	Three Waltzes for pianoforte	G flat major
	1843	,,	... ...	F minor
	1830	,,	... ...	D flat major
71	1827	1855	Three Polonaises for pianoforte	D minor
	1828	,,	... ...	B flat major
	1829	,,	... ...	F minor
72	1827	1855	Nocturne for pianoforte	E minor
	1829		Marche Funèbre for pianoforte	C minor
	1830		Three Écossaises for pianoforte	D major, G major, and D flat major
73	1828	1855	Rondo for Two pianofortes	C major
74	Dates ranging from 1829-1847	1855	Seventeen Polish Songs	

IV.—THOSE PUBLISHED POSTHUMOUSLY WITHOUT OPUS NUMBER.

Date of Composition.	Date of Publication.	Title.	Key.
1824	1851	Variations on a German Air, for pianoforte	E major
1825	...	Mazurka for pianoforte	G major
1825	...	Do. do.	B flat major
1829-30	...	Do. do.	D major
1832	...	A revised version of the preceding Mazurka	D major
1833	...	Mazurka for pianoforte	C major
...	...	Do. do.	A minor
...	1868	Waltz for the pianoforte	E minor
1822 (?)	1864	Polonaise for the pianoforte	G sharp minor
...	1872	Polonaise for pianoforte (published by B. Schott & Sons)	G flat major
1826	...	Polonaise for pianoforte	B flat minor
1829	...	Waltz for pianoforte	E major

If the number of times of performance of the different works at Messrs. Chappell's Monday and Saturday Concerts can in any way be taken as evidence of their popularity, the following list may prove interesting. It contains all those works of Chopin performed more than once at these concerts from February 14th, 1859, to March 23rd, 1891 :—

Title.	Number of times of performance.
Barcarolle in F sharp minor, Op. 60,	16
Introduction and Polonaise, Op. 3,	14
Ballade in G minor, Op. 23,	11
Impromptu in F sharp major, Op. 36,	10
Ballade in A flat,	9
Scherzo in B flat minor, Op. 31,	9
Polonaise in F sharp minor, Op. 44,	8
Polonaise in A flat major, Op. 53,	7
Scherzo in B minor, Op. 20,	7
Nocturne in D flat, Op. 27,	7
Sonata in B minor, Op. 58,	6
Fantasia in F minor, Op. 49,	5
Trio in G minor (violin, violoncello, piano), Op. 8,	4
Sonata in G minor (piano and 'cello), Op. 65,	4
Nocturne in F minor, Op. 55,	4
Nocturne in E major, Op. 62,	4
Andante Spianato and Polonaise, Op. 22,	3
Ballade in F minor, Op. 52,	3
Berceuse in D flat major, Op. 57,	3
Sonata in B flat minor, Op. 35,	3
Valse in A flat major, Op. 42,	3
Rondo for two pianofortes, Op. 73,	2
Allegro de Concert, Op. 46,	2
Nocturne in F major, Op. 15,	2
Nocturne in C minor, Op. 48,	2
Nocturne in C sharp minor,	2
Valse in C sharp minor, Op. 64,	2
Valse in E minor (posthumous),	2

INDEX